Demon Crossfire

The Enoch Wars, Book 3

By Ben Settle

Published by Neanderthal Publishing, Inc.

ISBN: 1519415583
ISBN-978-1519415585

CRYPT OF CONTENTS

INTRODUCTION

It's quite an honor to write *Demon Crossfire*'s introduction.

I've written intros before, but never for a fiction title. Certainly never for such a quality novel as *Demon Crossfire.*

I'm biased though. Perhaps I'm not the best person to write this introduction. I'm biased because I enjoyed the draft manuscript of the first *Enoch Wars* book so much, the acclaimed *Zombie Cop*, that I demanded that Ben let my company publish it under our imprint, Neanderthal Publishing (a subsidiary of MakeRight Publishing, Inc., naturally).

If Ben had denied my demand, he wouldn't have had a moment of undisturbed sleep the rest of his days. Had he chosen another publisher, I'd be lurking in the shadows of every dark alley he walked past making him rue the day he first heard my name.

(Upon re-reading that, well…that might be sort of weird. So maybe I wouldn't have stalked him the rest of his life. But you can bet good money that I would have sent him a sternly-worded email.)

So now we already have a trilogy. One that will result in a seven-book series before *The Enoch Wars* readers enjoy the final word.

So far, we have:

Zombies in *Zombie Cop*

Vampires in *Vampire Apocalypse*

And now demons; real *bad* demons.

Along the way, we get a glimpse at more than one Predator, a few werewolves tossed in for good measure, and we've learned in these first three stories that Ben's a master at dropping hints along the way of future things to come.

I have no doubt other monsters are going to join the fun before long. (Perhaps an archangel or some similar being will join in from the other side as well. Who knows what lurks in the heart of a Benjamin Settle?)

Ben Settle Tells Far Better Stories than Mega-Producer J. J. Abrams

The statement above is simple to prove.

To do so, all I have to do is quote an email that a famous author sent to Ben last month after reading an early draft of *Demon Crossfire.* I won't use the Author's name here, but I promise you that *each* and *every one of you* have read his writing:

"… Ben, your writing is becoming powerful, removing the sense of reading words far quicker than ever before. By this, I mean most readers will be closely following the story without feeling as though they are *reading* a story. *That* is the sweet spot fiction writers desire but rarely achieve.

"In the past decade and a half, television writing has improved dramatically. Still, they fall into a trap so often when they go on too long: they start making up back story mid-series to bring in connected characters and plots that don't fit with the first several seasons. *NCIS* was fantastic its first six years, because from the very beginning they gave hints on back story that they often didn't explain until three, four, or even five seasons later. *Breaking Bad* was the King of this because *Breaking Bad* knew where it was headed from the start. The producers and writers knew the ending and all the major characters' conclusions before the pilot episode aired. They never had to make up backstory because they didn't drag their show past the backstory sweet spot. I won't mention any names of the bad ones. Okay, I will: *Lost, Alias, Person of Interest, Lost* (whose final seasons were so bad, it's worth mentioning twice), and *The Blacklist* (basically every show by Bad Robot's 2-seasons-and-I'm-stupid J. J. "Jar Jar" Abrams).

"It seems that Abrams expects his shows to get cancelled after two seasons so he never looks beyond the first season or two. If renewed for a third season, he has to start bringing in new 'old back story' plots to keep stretching new shows. It's an obvious plot device and always stretched too thinly. This is why all his shows start to stink near the end of their second season. Stink worse than Bruce Jenner's perfume.

"*You,* on the other hand, gave plenty of backstory from the first *Enoch Wars* book, *Zombie Cop*, to keep this series going through all seven planned novels. And you are masterful at bringing out those elements when needed, but until then, keeping them veiled with only minor references when not. *Demon Crossfire* does this so much, I was shocked at the story subplots that came out of mere tiny mentions from earlier books!

"Out of nowhere? Yep. Fits perfectly? Absolutely.

"*Demon Crossfire* is a superb story. Your best written.

"*Demon Crossfire* is far better in its third volume than any third season of any show J.J. Abrams has his hands on… as well as shows from many other producers and writers. You're a far better writer than anyone on those shows could hope to be.

"That says a lot considering how good your first two novels were."

Blasphemy, Pure Horror, or Uncanny Simple Truth?

What I have to say about *Demon Crossfire* needs to be put in context. For a while, I've been racking my brain trying to figure out a way to convey what I need you to know about this book. If you and I knew each other, I could personalize this introduction and explain in your terms why it's one of the most insightful novels written in the past five decades.

You're all strangers to me from mixed backgrounds though. So, the only way it's possible to describe what Ben's done, I believe, is for you to have insight into my psyche. *Then,* I think I can give you insight into Ben's psyche – or at least describe his book's amazing accomplishment.

So, please let me say something that'll cause most of you to hate me. (It'll only take a moment.)

I'm not a religious person. I'm a Christian.

Now, we're not talking about one of those good Christians you see in all the huge churches in America today. No, I'm one of the bad Christians.

I'm one of those judging Christians. You'll find me more often rebuking someone than lifting them up. After all, there's a lot to rebuke these days. And man, I'm a master at rebuking those who need it. Friends or strangers, just pass 'em my way and I'll take over from there.

Also, you know about us bad Christians, right? The ones "ignorant of science" who actually study the overwhelming scientific evidence that the earth is fewer than 7,500 years old? Yep. Me again.

Now you have context on what I'm about to say. You might not believe the Bible is true. That's fine. (As Putty once told Elaine, "I'm not the one going to hell.") What does matter is that you understand I know what's in that big book gathering dust on all of today's good Christians' shelves. I'm well versed in its verses.

Demon Crossfire is a book I love, not only for its pure, fun, horrorific storytelling but for what's between the lines. Between the lines, *Demon Crossfire* exposes and emasculates weak, religious, good Christians today. If you, like me, don't like good Christians, then in *Demon Crossfire* we have a common enemy: phony religious people. Ben eviscerates them without ever once sounding preachy.

As a matter of fact, most will finish this book and not know what I'm talking about. That is good. Writing that has special, hidden treasures for only a few of its readers is the best writing.

I was blown away by Ben's tremendous insight into people, especially religious people.

So, if you're an atheist then you'll love how Ben exposes the phonies. If you're a bad Christian who's judgy and anti-choice, then you'll love how Ben exposes the phonies. If you're a good Christian today, you won't have a clue. (But you'll still like the book.)

Fun, Horrible, Crude, and Bible Aren't Synonyms – But They're All Here!

Demon Crossfire is a major milestone in Ben Settle's writing.

Demon Crossfire is a major milestone in the genre of horror fiction.

The story is everything for everybody. (Try pulling *that* off, Stephen King!)

People who would never read such a book, should read this one.

People who love such books will realize by about the third chapter how much more there is here than typically found in the average, horror story.

Ben's nailed another one. In each *Enoch Wars* volume, Ben ups the game. When he told me he had a follow-up to the first one, *Zombie Cop*, I expected it to be weak. How could he top *Zombie Cop*? When newly-minted Zombie, Chief Rawger, told his two little girls to come to daddy... well, you know they were going to get a hug to die for.

Then, in *Vampire Apocalypse*, Ben didn't just up the game, he boosted it to new heights. The vampire who'd lived hundreds of years, Fezziwig, an avid fan of *Miami Vice*'s fourth season (the misunderstood season), trying to get to the airport with his prostate acting up, the sun pounding down, and his concubine on the fritz, is a reading pleasure rarely enjoyed. *Vampire Apocalypse*'s audiobook narrator had to stop and repeat section after section of chapter 2 due to his breaking up in unrestrained laughter, taking three full sessions to record what would normally take only a half session.

How could Ben do better than that? Answer: *Demon Crossfire.*

The writing is even *more* advanced, the sarcasm throughout is somehow *more* side-splitting than before, and the element you read about earlier – the educated insight into good, religious phony Christians today – oh man.

Babe Ruth couldn't hit one out of the park with more finesse than Ben's done here.

But you didn't buy the book to read me. (Seriously, we didn't charge you any extra for this Introduction.) So turn the page and prepare to travel on a journey like no other. Join me in quickly finding the answer to the obvious question: "How can Ben possibly top the first two books?"

Sincerely offered,
Greg Perry, Publisher

"Now the giants, who have been born of the spirit and the flesh, shall be called upon the earth evil spirits, and on the earth shall be their habitation. Evil spirits shall proceed from their flesh, because they were created from above; from the holy watchers was their beginning and primary foundation. Evil spirits shall they be upon earth, and the spirits of the wicked shall they be called.""

- Enoch 15:8-9

1
LUCIFER'S TAMPON

"The jig is up, the news is out
They've finally found me.
The renegade who had it made retrieved for a bounty.
Never more to go astray,
This will be the end today of the wanted man."

- Styx
Renegade

- 1 -

"I can't tell if you're a dude or a chick or just another one of these ugly trannies popping up lately," said Azriel Creed. "But you're obviously not *human.* So I guess that means no restraint necessary."

Azriel wasted no time. The moment the tall mannish-looking woman with the Chicago Cubs hat and Green Bay Packers socks sat next to him at the bar and threatened to kill him, he punched her face. Azriel pulled back his closed fist and rubbed it. He had just hit her with enough force to smash through a brick wall. He was feeling noticeably stronger every day since his fight with the vampires 15 months earlier.

"You think you can stop me with a love tap?" the man-chick said with her mysterious accent. She flashed Azriel a bloody, toothless smile, and swallowed hard. Her two dislodged front teeth raced down her throat. Azriel noticed a couple thick scars, like teeth marks, on her neck. But not vampire fang marks. They looked more like canine teeth.

Azriel assumed the man-chick was a Predator like him. Both were of an ancient race of supernaturally strong people bred from Biblical times to hunt down and kill the monstrous offspring created by fallen angels mating with human women. She had to be one of his kind. There was no other explanation. For one, she didn't activate his internal alarm system that sounded in his gut whenever a monster was nearby. And also, his punch's force would have required any regular person to eat from a straw for life — assuming they didn't die on impact.

"You aren't strong enough yet to kill me, little Predator. Today I am the monster, and you are the prey."

The man-chick stood up.

Her seven-foot plus tall body cast a shadow over Azriel's short stature.

Azriel dived for her legs.

The man-chick lifted her knee towards his face and tagged him in his nose — knocking him onto his back. Blood poured out of his nose and into his hands. The man-chick reminded Azriel of the way Granny fought. She moved in much the same way. He wondered if all the other Predators knew how to fight except him.

Azriel's blood splattered on the floor. He heard the tavern owner, Jackson, yelling something about calling the police and to take it outside.

The man-chick laughed.

Her laugh was a deep, baritone sound.

"I thought this would be harder, Azrael" she said. "Lucifer's favorite? With all your bleeding you look more like Lucifer's *tampon.*"

Azriel's head spun. He sniffed the blood back into his nose, wiped the rest with his finger, and stood back up.

The man-chick smiled. "Time to die little devil tampon," she said. She reached into her left sock and pulled a large syringe out. The syringe was full of a blue liquid. She slid the plastic needle-head covering off and lightly pressed on the plunger. A few blue drops plopped onto the floor next to her feet. She jerked her feet away from where the drops hit, as if she was dodging acid. "Nasty substance," she said. "I hate even being near it. But it will make killing you more… *efficient.*"

Just being near the drops that hit the floor made Azriel feel woozy. His nose felt as if it were broken. Blood continued to gush from it down his face and onto the wood floors.

"This has been used to kill our kind for thousands of years," said the man-chick. "Just touching this syringe makes me feel *sick.*"

Azriel's heart started beating faster.

He knew exactly what was in that syringe:

It was the same substance in the blue pills Pastor Shane had given him during his childhood. It suppressed his abilities and made him feel violently ill if he even so much as thought about squashing a bug, much less committing violence.

Blue pills. Balls!

\- 2 -

The man-chick had Azriel pinned on the floor with her knee on his chest before he could process another thought. He swung and reached at her tree trunk-like legs. She smiled and put the syringe in her mouth sideways with one hand. With her other hand, she socked Azriel's face over and over again.

The man-chick's hands were gigantic. Her nails were dry and bitten down.

Each of her punches felt like it had broken something in Azriel's face. He felt his nose shatter, his teeth bust, his jaw rattle, and his eyes puff and swell.

"Quit *squirming*," mumbled the man-chick with the syringe in her mouth. "If you make this easy, I might kill you quickly. If you keep making it difficult, I will make you suffer. Understand?"

She stopped hitting Azriel, grabbed his neck with her left hand, and punched him in his solar plexus with her right. Azriel struggled to suck in air.

"That's better," said the man-looking chick grabbing the syringe out of her mouth.

Azriel struggled to breathe. The man-chick kept her hand on Azriel's neck. She squeezed so tight he couldn't get any oxygen in even if he hadn't had the wind knocked out of him.

Azriel gasped and heaved, waiting for the wind in his system to return. He was already starting to heal from her blows, and noticed her two front teeth had mostly grown back. The fast-healing they both shared was a blessing and curse when fighting each other. He couldn't help but think, again, he really needed to learn how to fight. Rage and violent intent weren't enough as he discovered with Rawger, Rood, Fezziwig, Granny, and even Finius. No matter how strong he was, no matter how fast, no matter how angry… it was all for nothing if his opponents out fought him. But he didn't know any formal ways of fighting. It was all instinct.

"You ready to die, little devil *tampon*?"

The man-chick smiled and showed Azriel the syringe. A blue drop emerged from the needle tip. The man-chick jabbed the needle into Azriel's jugular and emptied half the syringe's contents into his vein. "No need to waste all of it," she laughed, "just a dab will do you!"

She stood up, wiped her mouth, and grinned.

- 3 -

Azriel's body flooded with a familiar rush of nausea and pain.

He felt as if he was going to puke out the light lunch he'd eaten while drafting the short story about the owl with insomnia right before this bitch sat next to him.

Azriel lay on the floor in a fetal position. He knew he needed to try and calm himself. Thinking of violence or fighting or even swearing (*does thinking "balls!" count…?*) now debilitated him. He pressed on the switch in his brain over and over. That switch had been endlessly useful. It let him mind-control zombies and turn vampires into bats. It had also sometimes helped alleviate the intense pain the blue pills caused.

"If you'd held still I would have let you die quickly," said the man-chick. "I would have ripped your puny head off and granted you mercy. But you had to keep struggling, didn't you? You just couldn't die like a good little monster. So now I'm going to make you suffer. *She* will finally be proud of me when I show her your head."

The man-chick kicked Azriel in the ribs.

He heard two of them snap like they were a couple of dry twigs.

"Painful isn't it?" the man-chick said. "I once was injected with this. The man who did it said where it came from — the top of Mount Hermon. All the way in the Holy Land. He said it was used originally to take down the *first* Predator who— "

"Just kill me already… fuck it, I'm done with this shit life," said Azriel, squirming in pain. His head felt like a thousand pins were impaling his skull. His stomach felt like something was inside chomping on his organs, and about to pop out like in the *Alien* movies.

"All in due course, little devil tampon," said the man-chick. "There are so few of us left. I take no pleasure in killing another of our kind. But I do take pleasure in killing *you*. It's an honor to kill Lucifer's favorite. She will finally approve!"

Who's "she"? And what's with this Lucifer's favorite gag?

Fezziwig called Azriel the same title.

What the hell did it mean?

The question stuck in Azriel's mind even amidst the pain while he lay on the sticky tavern floor which smelled like alcohol and salt and lemon. *I could go for one of Jackson's margaritas right about now,* came a stray thought.

Azriel heard police sirens and saw the strobe lights reflecting off the waxed floor.

Jackson must have called them.

"Dammit. I wanted to make you suffer," said the man-chick noticing the cops outside. "I am out of time."

She walked over to the bar, reached behind it, and grabbed a long serrated knife. "Dismemberment is messy enough even with the right tools. I should have brought my own. No matter."

She kneeled down to Azriel's body, grabbed his hair with one hand, and put the long knife to his throat to decapitate him alive. She stared into Azriel's eyes as if fascinated by the idea of watching the life leave him.

"A power saw would be more efficient. But this will have to do…"

The man-chick smiled as she prepared to cut Azriel's head off.

- 4 -

The man-chick pressed the blade down on Azriel's neck but was stopped by a pair of strong fingers digging into the back of her neck so hard they felt like they would puncture her skin.

They were Azriel's fingers.

She glanced down at Azriel's eyes and saw him wink just before two other fingers darted into her own eyes so hard she thought they'd go straight to the back of her skull. She dropped the knife and leaned back, pulling the thin, strong fingers out of her eye orbits. As she struggled to regain her vision Azriel head-butted her, knocking her to floor.

Azriel didn't know how to fight formally.

But, he did know how to fight *dirty*.

He hopped to his feet, picked up a bar stool, and smashed it over the man-chick's head. As her eyesight started to return he got around her and punched her as hard as he could in her spine. He heard something snap and she slumped to the floor, screaming. Azriel picked the knife up and impaled her left bicep with it directly into the floor. The knife must have been stainless steel, he figured. A cheap knife would have broken over her strong skin.

The man-chick cried out.

Blood gathered by her arm in a pool as she rubbed her eyes with her free hand.

Azriel scanned the ground.

Where was it?

Where did the bitchy butch put it?

The man-chick grabbed the knife handle and pulled it out of her arm and the floor. She raised herself up to the bar. She then grabbed a handful of napkins and plugged up the wound. The napkins went from white to red in seconds.

Now who's the tampon, *Butch?* thought Azriel, followed by, *Where the hell is it?*, as he continued to scan the ground.

There it is!

Got it!

The man-chick regained her composure, breathed in, and leaped towards Azriel, whose back was turned to her on his knees on the ground. She had the knife held in such a way where she was going to plunge it right into the top of his skull.

- 5 -

As the man-chick's knife was about to sink into Azriel's skull he turned towards her, grabbed her wrist attached to the hand with the knife in it, and stabbed her eyeball with the same blue liquid-filled syringe she injected him with.

He emptied the rest of it into her eye.

She fell onto the ground on her back, syringe still stuck in her pupil.

She gasped and vomited, wriggling on the floor screaming and crying. Tears streamed down her face. She tried to take the syringe out of her eye but was too weak to even do that.

Azriel stood over her.

His 5-foot-6 skinny frame was erect and strong — as if the blue pill liquid that had debilitated him had never entered his blood stream just seconds earlier.

"Well aren't you just a sight for sore *eyes*?" said Azriel using his foot to push the syringe deeper into her eyeball.

He watched her squirm around in the pool of blood created from the wound in her arm and smiled. For whatever reason, the blue pill substance wasn't effecting him anymore. Mere moments after she injected him the pain went away, completely.

If anything, he felt *stronger.*

- 6 -

Azriel noticed the squad car strobe lights outside again.

Balls.

The police are going to be in here any second.

I need information from this bitch.

Azriel looked out the blinds. There were two squad cars. DaBeach only had two cops — both part time — and they were both here. It was probably the most excitement they'd had in years. Certainly it was a welcome distraction from their usual calls of finding some meth-head Highway 101 drifter passed out in a public bathroom or a petty vacation home burglary. Azriel could see the cops standing outside their cars talking to Jackson. They both had a hand on their holstered guns.

"Okay you cunt," said Azriel. "Tell me what I want to know and I'll kill you *fast.* Jerk me around and I'll drag you into the woods, and see what I can stick in your other eye. Get it?"

The man-chick nodded. She was lying in a fetal position. One arm was holding her bleeding belly holding her guts in, the other rubbing her temple being inundated with intolerable waves of pain pulsating through her head. The needle was still sticking in her eyeball.

"Who sent you? Who is sending Predators to kill me and why?"

"You are Lucifer's favorite. He has plans for you… to use you."

"For what?"

"Death. Destruction. Armageddon. He knows who your *father* is. What you are capable of. Roper said…"

"Who the hell is Roper?"

"Leader."

"Leader of what?"

"The Order."

Azriel heard the tavern door creak open. Time was running out.

"Where can I find this Roper?"

The man-chick smiled. "Mount Rainier, Maryland. Go there. Go now. I hope you find him. He will kill you himself!" She winced as another wave of pain and nausea shot through her body.

"Thanks," said Azriel. He then plunged the knife into her heart and face and her other eye several times, until the knife blade broke off while inside her chest. He watched her slump over, completely still.

- 7 -

Azriel ran out the back door just before the two officers were all the way inside. He watched from the window as they knelt beside the man-chick and could hear one of them on his radio calling for an ambulance.

They should be calling the morgue instead, thought Azriel.

He ran towards the small beach cabin he rented a half mile away. His superhuman attributes allowed him to run faster than a speeding car and he made it there in seconds. He grabbed a big duffel bag out of the closet and tossed some clothes and any non-perishable food he could find into the bag.

He heard the ambulance in the distance.

He smiled again, amused. *I don't think CPR is gonna quite cut it, boys. And who would give that ugly bitch CPR anyway…*

When Azriel was all packed he grabbed a United States map and left. He felt guilty for not letting his landlord Tony know. He liked the guy. The man was always nice to him, even invited him to have dinner with him and his wife one time. But Azriel, being a recluse, declined. He could tell it offended his landlord. But so it was with regular people. They simply didn't understand his hatred of social pleasantries and small talk.

No time to care about that now.

No time to think about how much he was going to miss living on that beach, and having some measure of peace for the first time in his entire life. It was the best nine months he ever had.

But he knew peace was not his destiny.

People like him died brutal, painful deaths.

He'd even dreamed of it happening — where he was burning in a furnace with invisible entities laughing and cheering it on. At least he thought it was him in the dream, but he couldn't be sure.

And like it or not, it was time to leave DaBeach, as much as he loved living there. The only thought on his mind now was how this Roper asshole, who kept sending Predators to kill him, was already dead.

The dude just didn't know it yet.

2
THE TERRIBLE ONE

"Did they give you an anal probe?"

- Chef
Southpark

- 1 -

The arch demon Rapha was starving when he escaped the abyss while the vampire and half zombie battled.

The gnawing hunger was unlike anything he had felt since he was in a flesh giant body thousands of years earlier. In life he was the child of a fallen angel and a mortal woman. He stood 12-feet tall and was regarded as the smartest of all Nephilim. His superhuman intellect and strength designed and built the great Egyptian pyramids and Easter Island monuments. And during his long life he spawned a tribe of giants his enemies called the *Rephaim* — meaning "The Terrible Ones" — after his own name.

Rapha's immediate mission was to destroy Lucifer's favorite.

Abaddon told Rapha and the arch demon Arba, who left the pit with him, it was their one and only mission. It was the sole reason they were being released after 2,000 years. But as the two demons escaped the pit, they saw the boy Predator was already dead. The vampire had completely drained his body of blood. At that point, Rapha decided to focus on the one all-consuming pain he had:

Hunger.

The moment he left the pit he, like all demons, craved embodiment. But in this case, even more urgent than embodiment, he needed to *feed*, first.

He craved the taste of human fear.

And terror.

And despair.

Rapha rarely outright killed anyone when he was a Nephilim giant. And it was the same after he died and became a disembodied demon. He enjoyed humiliating, dominating, and tormenting his enemies for weeks, and months, and years, before allowing them to die. He particularly liked to lecture them about philosophy, math, and the probabilities of various irrelevant events happening while torturing his captives. He relished using the biggest and most complicated words he could think up to explain the mathematics behind how he and his Rephaim tribe designed and constructed the pyramids. How he aligned them precisely with the stars, fallen angel end-time strategy, and spiritual warfare. He enjoyed having that "captive audience" as he called his victims.

In those days Rapha was notorious for thinking up new and exciting ways to torture his enemies. His favorite was what the ancient world called "flaying." He carefully placed a wooden stake inside an enemy's anus and hammered it in so precisely it only just pushed the internal organs aside — causing intolerable agony, infection, and internal bleeding. Some of his victims suffered for days and weeks like this — tortured by the intense pressure and stretching of their orifice. And the whole time Rapha would casually talk to his victims about such trivial matters as the flaws in the code of Hammurabi or the unintended consequences caused by newest forms of Egyptian irrigation.

These things pleasured Rapha's sick psyche in life. And after his flesh giant body died, they sustained his disembodied demonic appetites in death, too. After being cast into the abyss by Jesus Himself (when no other holy man could do it) he spent the last two thousand years being tormented himself by the fallen angels trapped inside.

But Rapha was free now thanks to Abaddon's vampire son holding the abyss door open just long enough for him to slip out. And since his mission to destroy Lucifer's favorite had been completed by the vampire, Rapha was free to terrorize once again. He just needed to *eat*, first, he realized, as he made his way north towards the nearest, brightest beacon of negative energy and pain he could find:

A city called "Elgin."

A strange name, he thought.

What does it mean?

Perhaps when he embodied someone and learned current vernacular, historical events, and changes in technology during the last 2,000 years, he would know.

But before embodiment, he would feed.

He probed the area looking for a crack to slip into and exploit someone with torment and anguish and feast like the king he once was.

- 2 -

Rapha wandered downtown Elgin disembodied and hungry.

He briefly inhabited and read the minds of random people walking by who all felt a strong sense of despair and horror. This was how most human men and women reacted in a demon's presence. Their hairs stood up straight and goose flesh popped up on their bodies. They felt an impending sense of cold, dread, hopelessness, and despair. Many times they smelled sulfur, too.

To possess a person or enter a home he either needed to be invited, or he had to find a crack to slip in through. Most cracks were spiritual in nature. Like cursed objects, pagan idolatry, or opening doorways that loosened the connection between a person's spirit and their brain — such as hypnosis, or divinations, or trying to "summon" or communicate with beings such as himself. Once inside, he could raid the fridge of the home's inhabitants' negative emotions and feed, turning them on each other, and ultimately drive them to murder, suicide, and destruction.

Most of the people in this town had more than one small crack through which he could enter their minds to possess them. Some of them had hundreds of cracks. Some were more like gaping holes. But, as in the old days, there were always people he couldn't inhabit. They had the Holy Spirit in them. Rapha was as repulsed by them as men were by him. Each human had a spiritual scent. And people with the Holy Spirit smelled rancid. It vexed Rapha to even be near them.

Fortunately for Rapha, most of the people in this town didn't have the Holy Spirit. Even the priest who walked down the street smiling and shaking peoples' hands had cracks to slip in through. At a glance, Rapha expected the priest to be especially revolting. But he wasn't. He smelled sweet and tasty. Rapha inhabited him, read his mind, and saw what he truly was: a man with no conscience who stole money from his congregation, fucked and impregnated married women, secretly encouraged those women to murder their unborn children while preaching openly against such atrocities, and kept hidden stashes of deranged pornography hidden under the church pews. The priest loved the thrill of the idea of his flock sitting on top of the filth and never suspecting.

Oh how Rapha *liked* the world now!

Even many of the priests were lost!

Not even the Baal-worshipers of old were this diabolical!

Rapha realized he had somewhat of a pleasant problem:

It wasn't a matter of finding a crack to slip in through like in the old days.

No.

It was a matter of *which* crack to pick from.

A delectable problem to have indeed!

The earth was like a demonic banquet table. Back when he walked the earth as a flesh giant, he and the other Nephilim tribes — giants and monsters alike — committed many acts that turned mankind's stomachs. Most of them were *sexual* in nature. But Rapha and his Nephilim cousins knew they were doing evil. They even used sex — wicked, evil sex acts on animals and family members — as worship to their fallen angel fathers. It was done in the open, blatantly, and with full knowledge, even boasting of their evil acts. The more evil and wicked, the more they were feared and respected. The beauty of today, Rapha realized, was men do evil but think they are doing *good.*

This holy man has even convinced himself he's doing God's work.

Such was Rapha's pleasant problem:

Yes, he could feed, but it was what these people today called "empty calories." Men and women embraced their depravity. It was like eating stale fast food. It sustained him, but had no satisfaction. No taste. No enjoyment. And he was hungry immediately after. A demon's sustenance didn't come from making the terminal dead or sicker. It was in taking the healthy and making them terminal with despair, and anguish, and turning them away from their Creator.

Rapha was getting hungrier by the minute and snacking wasn't enough. He needed a full meal. But who should he feast on first?

He soon found the answer right in front of him.

Of course!

Perhaps the best "crack" of all for a demon looking to torment innocent people:

Generational.

Generational curses were huge doorways.

No resistance.

No needing an invitation to get inside the home.

The sins of the parents are a deliciously succulent commodity indeed, Rapha thought, as he saw a husband and wife with a small child entering a car.

The family was plainly marked with such a curse and Rapha followed them inside.

- 3 -

Rapha hovered in the back seat next to the child.

The first thing he learned reading the parent's minds was they had no spiritual covering. They went to church to socialize and be entertained. They liked the music and the pastor was a good orator. But they weren't fed anything. The pastor never even mentioned the son of God's name in his sermons. These two would be easy pickings. Conversely, the child was only five years old, sweet, innocent, and loving. He had only pure thoughts. But that didn't matter since he was part of the generational curse and was open game.

Rapha decided to save the child's suffering for last.

Dessert, he thought.

During the ride the couple complained about feeling cold, nervous, and depressed. And what was with that God-awful rotten egg smell? They argued, accused each other of trivial things, and were uneasy the entire way.

It amused Rapha how human selfishness was greater today than it was more than 2,000 years ago. The parents did not even notice the child had not moved or even blinked the entire ride home. Rapha was reading the child's spirit and the generational curse the three had. He saw both the man and woman had parents who were involved in witchcraft — always a wide open doorway.

This particular version of witchcraft was called *Wicca.*

A stupid name, Rapha thought. *Sounds like the name of a basket.*

When they got home Rapha found numerous cursed objects. Some were bought off a site called *eBay*. And others were handed down from the couples' witch-parents. Rapha enjoyed reading the various objects — a sapphire necklace heirloom which had been used in demon-summoning rituals… a vase that had been used to drink the blood of sacrificed children… a dollhouse once used to hide a body part of a murdered nun… a stuffed doll with a suicide victim's hair.

They were so bound up in generational curses they were *ripe* for the picking.

Of course, Rapha was only too happy to take advantage of the situation…

- 4 -

Rapha decided to do something special to this family.

It had been too long since he had this kind of fun. He wanted to torment them with life-long anguish he could feast on now and later whenever he got hungry and wanted a good meal or just to snack. Rapha didn't have the power and abilities to do it exactly like his angelic father did — who gave humans visions and experiences so real they couldn't tell the difference between fantasy and reality. No, demons had that kind of power. But being an arch demon, Rapha could alter perception to the point where he could do a *passable* job at it. At the very least, he would have some fun and eat well watching the family wallow in despair.

Rapha watched the man and woman put their child to bed.

The child didn't fall asleep right away.

He looked nervous.

As the man and woman climbed into their own bed in the other room, both complaining of a draft and about how they should see their doctor about anti-anxiety medication, Rapha watched them have their tepid sex. The man entered his wife on top. He told her how her hair smelled fresh and her eyes were the most beautiful things he'd ever seen.

If Rapha had solid food in his stomach he would have wretched it up.

It was revolting to him.

He wondered if all men today were so passive and timid. The woman pretended to like the sex with fake moans. But Rapha could see her boredom and near-disgust at the man mounting her, as he asked for her permission to kiss her, touch her, and fuck her.

In Rapha's day, men *commanded* their women to fuck. Men pulled their women's hair and grabbed their throats and bit them, not compliment them and ask for permission.

Mankind has become so… unimaginative… in my absence, Rapha thought.

He decided it was something he would have to remedy when he eventually possessed someone and indulged in all that host's fleshly sensualities.

But for now, as the couple fell asleep… the man thinking of his wife, the wife thinking of her husband's brother, Rapha prepared his feast.

- 5 -

The next morning the man and woman woke up naked and in pain.

The man's rectum was bleeding and the woman had bruises and needle marks around her puffy and swollen eyes. She was bleeding from her vagina and anus, and screaming about her baby being ripped out of her body and stolen.

Rapha fed on their fear and paranoia.

It tasted delicious.

He listened to the couple — amidst their surprise and hysteria — mention how the house was still cold no matter how high the thermostat was. And why was that rotten eggs smell still lingering? They couldn't account for up to 6 hours of the night after they had sex. They were exhausted, scared, and near ready to have a nervous breakdown.

Rapha ate hearty of all these emotions.

They tasted better than even the flesh of the man he ate while alive as a giant, when he was starving in the wilderness. That day Rapha savored every swallow and scream as he chomped on the man's legs and arms, tearing off and swallowing one limb at a time, using tight string and rope to cauterize the wounds so his victim-meal wouldn't bleed out and die too soon.

But this was *different.*

This was way more exciting and tasty than anything he'd partaken of in life.

And he wanted more.

Ironically, the couple's experience was nothing compared to what Rapha had planned to do that night. But when the man shouted out the Son of God's deplorable Name, not even in belief but just as a cry, Rapha was forced to temporarily withdraw from the home. Luckily, the generational curses still made cracks for him to get back in to the home without needing to be invited. But he suspected the man yelled the Word out on accident anyway, and knew he didn't really believe in it. Thus, he calculated, the odds of the man yelling the Name again would be approximately 1,789 to 1.

The couple made a phone call after calming down. About an hour later a man with thick glasses, a tall hat, and dressed in a big coat showed up. The stranger started a recording device and then put the man and woman under hypnosis (*Could these fools possibly make this any easier on me?* laughed Rapha). The couple then told the man what happened that night, and what they had consciously forgotten:

They went to sleep and were awakened by their son crying out.

A bright light flooded in through their bedroom window. At first they thought it was the police or an emergency vehicle. Maybe the house next door was on fire?

The man tried to get up, but couldn't.

He was paralyzed.

So was the woman.

Their boy was screaming in the other room, but the parents could not move. The bedroom door, which was half way ajar, opened all the way. Three short gray humanoids with abnormally large bald heads and big eyes, and thin slits for mouths walked in. They were giggling. Their long fingers were pressed on their mouths. They spoke to the man and woman telepathically.

Don't be afraid. No harm will come to you. Don't be afraid. We're here to help you.

One of the creatures tossed the bed spread off. The three of them started touching the man and the woman all over their bodies and fondled their genitals.

Then there was a blinding white light.

The next thing the couple noticed was they were naked on cold metal tables. The room was white and dome-shaped. It reminded them of a sci-fi dentist's office. They saw strange looking medical instruments on tables next to them. Monitors were set up all around the room. A door across the room opened and the three gray humanoids walked in and circled the man's table. One stood on the man's right, one on his left, and one behind him. The couple could move and talk again. But they were still strapped on the tables unable to sit up or do more than wiggle their hands and feet.

The gray being on the man's left spoke:

Don't be afraid. We're here to help, it said as it held a long metal object up for the man to see. It spoke audibly, this time. The object was crusted with some kind brown substance that looked and smelled like shit.

"We will now commence with the physical examination. Worry not. There is an 18.764 percent chance you'll survive without any lasting infection."

One of the gray beings jabbed a long, sharp needle into the surface of the man's skin above his heart. Next, the being to his right produced a long syringe filled with a pale green liquid. The being moved it towards the man's neck, but the man resisted, twisting his head away. The gray being behind him spoke:

If you insist on resisting it will only accentuate the pain.

The being inserted the needle into the man's neck. The man started sweating and crying. He felt faint and tried to struggle.

All the gray beings took notes on clipboards. A light turned on. The man tried to move his head but couldn't. One of the beings brought the man a mask. The gray being put the mask over the man's mouth and nose. The man started feeling drowsy and everything went black. Before going under, he heard his wife screaming his name and pleading for the gray beings to stop. She asked them not to take her baby out of her body.

When the man awoke the gray beings were again fondling his genitals. Not in a perverted way. But in an indifferent, almost *mechanical* way.

More entities entered the room.

One was like a giant half man, half praying mantis.

Another was a half man, half grasshopper.

They both had two legs and two arms like men, but had the heads and flesh of insects. They made clicking noises. Like laughter. There was also a blonde man. He looked like something out of Norse mythology: tall and muscular, with blue eyes and blonde hair. It looked like someone Hitler would have called a perfect human specimen. He had a doctor's lab coat on and a clipboard.

The gray beings spread the man's legs and inserted the long, silver, brown substance-covered metal tube into his ass. The man screamed for help.

One of the gray beings held another long metal tube up. This one was longer than the last tube they put up his ass. It prepared to insert it in the man's rectum while the other object was still there. All the entities laughed. The gray being put its fingers to its mouth as if giggling while it prepared to insert the tube.

Then… terrified to the point of almost blacking out… the man yelled a name. Even under hypnosis the man didn't remember what the name was. That part of the night was mysteriously cloudy. But the man insisted that immediately after he yelled the name the anal probe was withdrawn and the next thing he remembered was waking up.

Despite the hypnosis, the man's wife had no recollection of the night before. But her vagina was sore and enlarged. It looked like she had just given birth. Her eyes were hurting, and she felt no boogers or mucous in her nose, like it had been sucked out by a vacuum. She felt a sharp pain in her brain and a sense of loss and sadness.

When the couple finished telling their story, the man in the big coat stopped writing and turned off the recording device.

He said, "You've been visited."

"By what?" asked the woman.

"The aliens. Grays. Isn't it fascinating?"

- 6 -

Rapha had never had so much *fun.*

He had heard the angels in the pit tell stories of doing this sort of thing to people when they had visited earth in the old days — both before and after the great flood. In life, as a giant, and later when he died and became a demon, Rapha never had been able to induce this kind of fear.

The fear he induced then was mere terror.

But this was a different kind of emotion.

It was much *tastier.*

It was pure hopelessness.

The man and woman had no idea what to do. They knew the horrors of the last night were just the beginning. The man in the coat — a "researcher" he called himself — was just as bound up in demonic footholds as the couple was. He was already pulling out various crystals from his coat.

"Here, take these," the man said.

"What are they?" asked the husband.

"Protection. These aliens have a *spiritual* aspect to them. They need to be warded off. And these crystals can do just that. Think of them like insect repellent and the aliens who attacked you are insects. It won't destroy them. But it will keep them at bay."

"This is crazy," said the wife holding her son close. "We were not visited by aliens. Someone slipped us some drugs or something!" The boy hadn't blinked the entire time.

The boy smiled, "They were my little *buddies*, mom" he said in a voice that echoed. The haunting sound made the three adults uneasy.

"What do you mean your little buddies? Do you remember what happened?" asked the man ignoring the researcher's request.

"There was a red light above my bed," said the boy's echoing voice. "The man in the light said not to be afraid. But I was afraid. But I was wrong. He is my buddy! We played all night together."

The man and woman looked at their son.

It didn't look like he'd been harmed.

Thank God for that, the husband and wife both thought.

"I was wrong. You are not in danger. Give me my crystals back!" said the man in the big coat snatching the crystals out of their hands. "I know what's going on now. Your boy is special. Maybe even *chosen.* Hear his voice? It's changed! Look at his eyes. The aliens have chosen him and wanted to examine you, his parents. Probably to see what makes your genetics tick. It's just good science. This is so exciting!" The man in the coat scribbled notes on a note pad as he spoke.

He then continued to tell the family what to do.

He said next time to let the aliens do whatever it is they are going to do. "Don't resist them. That is why they caused you pain," he said. "They want to *help* you. If you resist them next time, you will only anger them more. Let them take your boy aboard their mother ship. They will give him knowledge and wisdom. He's one of the children born in this generation who are going to usher in a new age of peace. One of the *indigo* children even maybe. Like the ones Oprah talked about."

Rapha was amused at how easily manipulated these people were. When he last wandered the earth as a demon nobody was this stupid.

When they went to bed, Rapha would induce more pain and fear on them. His original plan was to eat their despair, then he would leave them, then come back later and feast some more when he needed a snack. But he decided he was too hungry to leave leftovers behind. He wanted to not just feed but *feast.* And, he wanted to do it now. Tonight their fear would be joined with guilt, madness, and anguish.

The oven was pre-heating.

And he was going to dine well tonight.

- 7 -

The sun went down and the family got ready for bed. The man and woman had the boy sleep with them.

The man in the big coat with the crystals said they could expect another visitation. He did not know when, but he said it would probably be soon. They did not believe the man in the big coat nor were they going to let the so-called aliens take their child. They did believe the man in the big coat was right about one thing, though:

The family was *marked* now.

By what, exactly, they didn't know.

Aliens? Was the man retarded?

No, something else was afoot.

Something sinister.

Something spiritual.

They intuitively knew they could not hide from it or outrun it.

They spent the entire day on the Internet researching how to stop abductions but came up empty. It never occurred to them (to Rapha's amusement) to talk to their church pastor. Although, from what Rapha had seen of their pastor who didn't even use the son of God's name, he wouldn't be able to help and would likely just laugh if they heard the couple's story.

As they went to bed and the moon rose high in the sky, they saw the same lights flooding the bedroom windows. They wondered if the neighbors could see it.

Rapha prepared to torment them and feast on their anguish and despair.

This time he would let them believe he had anal probed all three of them.

He would stick things into their bodies, their genitals, and their brains while they slept, while influencing their dreams to think it was "aliens" doing it. He would feast on their fear and create an endless source of nourishment. Then he would make them kill the boy "for his own good," rationalizing it through their demon-possessed minds. Then they would kill themselves. And in that last moment when they decided to kill themselves, when their fear and guilt and anguish was at their worst… he would feed and feed and feed, relishing it like an orgasm.

Rapha prepared to do his worst.

Then, he stopped.

He felt another presence. It came into the home, was making its way up the stairs, and was now in the room.

Was it another demon?

Arba, maybe?

No.

This was something else.

He heard a crusted voice:

"Rapha."

"What do you want?" asked Rapha to the thing standing in the doorway. It was a pure black form — like a solid shadow. It had two glowing red eyes, long dangling arms, huge hands with sharp half-foot long claws, but no waist or legs. It hovered off the ground. It was so black it was darker than the darkness in the room. The man and woman and child could see its outline. For the first time the family heard Rapha's evil, icy voice. It terrified them to the bone.

"Abaddon has work for you to do," said the black shape.

"I am presently indisposed."

"Then get un-indisposed, idiot. Lucifer's favorite is still *alive*. You need to come with me. Dinner time is over."

The black shape looked at the family of three. Bright silver drool came out of his mouth, and hit the floor next to them.

"Well, *your* dinner is over," it said. "Mine is just starting." It licked its lips and opened its mouth wide.

3
HERO OF BAAL

"I never understood people's obsession with Ouija boards.
I don't even want to talk to the living."

- Greg Perry

- 1 -

After the arch demon Arba escaped the abyss, all he wanted to do was attack the vampire who robbed him of his prize.

Rapha was right in front of him, racing him to kill Lucifer's favorite. But the vampire had beat both demons to it. As soon as Arba escaped he saw the Predator's lifeless body on the ground — every drop of blood drained from it. The Predator was white as a corpse and just as still.

"Dammit!" said Arba as he fought off Rapha.

When Abaddon gave the two demons orders to kill Lucifer's favorite, he said the winner would be his first in command during Armageddon (with the loser to be tormented indefinitely), and Arba had no doubt he'd win. Arba knew Rapha's killing style was — as it was in life — slow and methodical, "chatty" as the other giant and monster tribes mocked. It was the opposite of Arba's fast and brutal style. Rapha spent his life hunting and torturing his enemies and using his supernatural intellect to build structures and monuments. But Arba spent his time conquering and pillaging. He usually gave his enemies a quick (but never painless) death. He didn't have time to play with his food. Nor did he like listening to their constant begging and pleading.

While Rapha wanted to torture and terrorize, Arba wanted to be king.

Nor did Arba care to savor his victim's emotions as Rapha did. Arba — whose name meant "Hero of Baal" in the ancient languages, due to his devotion to that fallen angel who also happened to be his father — was shorter than Rapha, but far more vicious. And Arba's tribe, called the *Anakim*, named after his son Anik, were Baal's greatest warriors. They conquered and killed just for the practicality of it, and not for the sport of it as Rapha's tribe did.

Arba wanted to kill that vampire for robbing him of his prize. But instead, the two demons fought each other right next to where the vampire and half zombie battled near the triangle-shaped abyss door. The two demons fought each other for miles in their disembodied forms. Just like with Rapha, Arba's demonic spirit and attributes were far stronger than most demons. And, also just like with Rapha, even Jesus's Disciples couldn't cast Arba out of people he possessed.

Eventually, the two demons grew tired of fighting.

What was the point?

They were hungry and thirsty, and in need of habitation.

So they parted ways.

Rapha decided to go north and Arba went south. They agreed to never interfere with each other again.

But Arba knew that was a lie.

He knew they would meet again. He would make sure of it. He was already plotting to gather other demons wandering the earth, form them into a tribe, and re-capture the planet as his giant clan almost had before.

But that was in the future.

His immediate need was food.

Arba didn't feel hunger in the abyss. Just despair. But now he felt hunger for others' despair. That was his food as a demon, he remembered, after 2,000 years of imprisonment. And he was famished. It did not take long for him to find a place where he could nourish himself.

He sensed what he needed in a town called "Carbondale."

He could smell the spiritual aroma of lust, and sin, and death all over. It was soothing. The first thing he noticed was how so many of the people gathered in bars and taverns and sweaty sex houses.

This will make an excellent feast, he thought. *And when feeding time is over, it's time to get to work killing Rapha.*

- 2 -

Arba was astonished at the town's abundance of food.

Most of the inhabitants were younger men and women — barely out of adolescence. He took his time briefly inhabiting people, reading their minds, and downloading their thoughts. As Arba read people's minds he caught himself up on the world, the new kinds of technology, historic events, the language, current vernacular, and the rampant spiritual decay. As a demon he could absorb people's thoughts. He could see their entire life history and events in a flash. He could read their experiences and feelings from the time they were in the womb to the present. He could see a person's entire life, everything their minds had seen, experienced, or recorded via their five senses. And in many of the people he saw plenty of cracks to slip in for possession.

Which one should he pick?

Which person to possess and feast on their despair first?

Carbondale's streets were packed with drunkards and young men trying to mate with girls who had no interest in them unless they had drugs or fame.

Boring, he thought.

It was nothing more than what these people called "fast food" for a demon.

Nothing to sink his teeth into.

Just small morsels.

He decided to try one of the nearby houses. He was in the mood to haunt, to feed on the fear and negative energy he would create, to ruin someone's life — all of which gave him sustenance and power. He felt the drive and need to conquer as much in death as a demon as he did in life as a giant king. It was his obsession. Haunting homes was the ultimate way for him to conquer now.

Arba stretched forth his demonic senses. He hoped to catch a scent of someone he could possess who would lead him to a real food source of negative emotions he could dine on.

It did not take long to find what he was looking for:

A home just outside of town near some woods.

The home had a dog. It barked and growled when Arba approached. Dogs and animals have senses humans don't, he remembered. There was a child inside the house who was not yet a teenager. She was a sweet, innocent girl. Arba's favorite kind of food. The trick was finding a spiritual crack in such a child so he didn't have to be invited inside. Invitations were hard to get, even from the deranged, sinful, and lost. But cracks were another matter. A crack would let him slip into a home undetected. And once inside this family could provide him all the despair he could eat. Fortunately, this child provided an easy crack for Arba to enter the house through:

She was trying to communicate with her dead mother.

Good girrrrrrl, Arba thought. *Inviting me in without having to ask…*

The child wanted to talk to her dead mother via a board — a *Ouija* board she called it — but was getting no answer.

Arba was more than happy to change that…

- 3 -

Arba spoke to the child posing as her dead mother throughout the entire night. It was like fattening up a meal of despair and terror.

The child's name was Blair.

Her dead mother's name had been Linda.

Blair was 13-years old, pathologically shy, loved pea soup, and had spoken to nobody else — not even her father — since her mother's body was found a week earlier. "I don't want to talk to anyone else, I just miss you so much mommy," she told Arba who was posing as her dead mother. Arba could read Blair's mind and knew just the right stories to tell, just the right words to say, and just the right way to say them.

Arba told her to keep their conversations private for now.

Your father won't understand. This is our little secret.

Humans were so naive.

It's why fallen angels had so easily seduced them centuries earlier. Plus this girl's faith in God was starting to fade. She had no spiritual covering. And, with Arba's voice haunting her and influencing her now, she no longer believed in God's Son whose Name Arba wouldn't even so much as think much less speak. This meant Arba would be able to pose as her mother, act as her god, and be her doom.

He decided first he would feed and grow strong on the negative energies and fear he would create in this home. Then he would destroy the girl and her father and her father's sister who was living with them. Then, he would go forth and conquer other demons on earth to create that army to kill Rapha and anyone else who got in his way. Such was his nature to be a king and ruler.

For now though, this was going to be fun.

Delicious fun.

Unholy and *unclean* fun.

- 4 -

The haunting began the next night.

When the girl, her father, and the father's sister were ready for sleep, and turning in — right at that time of night when everything always seems scarier and more horrific — Arba was upon them. The child Blair was trying to contact her mother again with the spirit board. But she would have to wait to talk to her. Arba was going to have some fun, first.

He floated down to the kitchen and opened the drawer. He could enter the material plane at will like that. His body — a grotesque looking mass, almost a humanoid form, but not quite — was invisible in the dark.

He knocked a glass onto the floor.

Then he turned on and off the lights.

Then he walked around, making his footsteps loud and deep on the wood floors. He broke a window and moaned aloud.

The father came down stairs, shotgun in hand, asking who was there. He was scared and shivering. His flesh was full of goose bumps and his hairs were standing up.

When the father saw the mess he called for Blair.

She was still on her board, trying to talk to her mother.

Arba raced upstairs to Blair's room.

Blair sensed Arba's presence the instant he entered.

That entire day, the home's inhabitants had complained of getting chills and feeling scared, and it smelled like rotten eggs. As Arba grew stronger, those sensations were accentuated. Arba's presence chilled Blair. But she was strangely attracted to the feeling now. And the longer Arba was around her and spoke to her, the more comfortable with the terror she became.

"You're here, Mom! You're back!" said Blair.

Arba whispered into her ear and left the room as the father came up. Arba could see their reflections in the mirror over the dresser. Blair stood up and looked at the mirror and spoke the first words she'd spoken to her dad in the week since her mother died:

"Mommy says she's coming back home soon! She has something special planned for us!"

The father scolded her and took her Ouija board away. Arba found that amusing. Once one such as he was let in, he could stay as long as he wanted, and would revisit whenever he wanted. Once you let a demon in there was only one way to keep it out. But this family didn't know that. If they had, Arba never would have been able to enter the home at all.

For the next few weeks Arba had his fun with the family.

He ate better than he had even in life as a giant clan king.

It was more Rapha's style to do things in this manner — slowly tormenting and terrorizing people. But Arba was enjoying himself and wanted to take his time. Conquering could wait. He had all the time in the world.

Arba started off with small hauntings:

Tapping the water pipes.

Breathing chilly breath in the father's or his sister's ear while they lay in their beds.

Even climbing into bed with Blair's father and lying next to him, feeling up his balls and cock in the exact same way his dead wife used to do. Whenever he was next to the father the man's heart raced, his flesh sweated, and he felt cold and scared. Blair's father knew something wasn't right and was always afraid. His dark hair even turned a shade of gray over the course of a few days. But he didn't want to think about it. Instead, he ignored it, suppressed it, and let his fear fester and grow. His daughter and his sister already had enough grief to deal with.

Good.

That makes it all the more tasty when he finally cracks…

Arba continued to tell Blair secrets each night. Including secrets about the man who killed her mother, what she was thinking when she died, the wicked things the killer did to her mother, how the killer enjoyed it, and how it was up to Blair to get revenge on him.

Then, after a week, Arba ramped it up. He was growing impatient. But it was like taking the time to prepare a feast versus eating fast food. It was worth the time and effort to spice his food up first.

Yes, it was definitely more Rapha's style.

But maybe Rapha wasn't such a fool after all?

Arba watched the father video skyping someone one night. He was alone in the house. Blair was away with her aunt. Arba stood right behind Blair's father, allowing his physical form to show. The person the father was talking to saw Arba through the computer screen and screamed, "Someone's in the room behind you!"

When the father turned, Arba was gone.

But there was a picture of his dead wife on the floor by his chair and the rotten egg smell was strong.

Blair's father screamed — unable to figure out how that photo made its way from the downstairs to the foot of his chair when he was alone.

The father's terror tasted so good to Arba.

When Blair got home that night with her aunt, Arba found the gold cross her mother was buried with, unearthed it, and put it on her bed. It still had a couple worms slithering around on it amongst the soil.

Blair's father was horrified. *How the hell did that get here?*

"I told you!" said Blair. "I told you she was coming back. This time she says she's taking us with her so we can all be together!"

Blair's father was happy his daughter was talking. But he was scared of *what* she was saying. Blair slept in her dad's room that night. All three were scared and had trouble relaxing. When they finally did sleep, Arba gave them nightmares by briefly inhabiting them and manipulating their thoughts. They saw in their dreams the man who murdered Blair's mother. His face was blurred out. They couldn't identify him. They watched him knock Linda out cold with a rag with some kind of chemical on it in a grocery store parking lot. He took her home and tortured her for days. Then he decapitated her, raped the corpse, and smiled at Blair and her dad, as if he knew they were watching him do his wicked deeds on camera.

In the morning Arba left a note on the end table:

ARE YOU EVER GOING TO AVENGE ME?

Blair, her dad, and her aunt screamed.

As they cried and screamed, Arba turned on the shower. The family members were petrified. Arba walked through shower and then walked out, leaving wet footprints in the hallways. All three of their hairs were standing up with goose flesh all over their bodies. The heat was turned up but they were still freezing. The rotten egg stench was especially strong.

That night Arba gave them another dream:

He made the two dream they were being attacked by the man who killed Linda. Arba strangled and attacked them all in their sleep, not letting them wake up. The next morning they each had hand prints on their necks and it hurt to swallow. Mysterious bruises were on their legs and stomachs and arms.

"That was it," declared Blair's dad.

He picked up the phone and called his minister who he hadn't seen in several years.

Perfect! thought Arba.

Now the real fun begins…

- 5 -

The minister immediately sensed something wrong in the home.

Arba smelled the lingering residue of the stench of God's spirit in him. But he had cracks in him. The minister was a drunkard and, at times, a womanizer, sleeping with whores on the side when taking trips to St. Louis as his aging wife became less attractive to him.

The minister would be easily dealt with.

He was even more of a boon to the plan than Arba had anticipated.

The minister anointed the home with olive oil and announced anything evil and negative inside to leave in the name of Jesus Christ.

Arba hated that name. It felt like a sharp pain in the side of his disembodied soul just hearing it spoken aloud.

He feared it more than anything else.

It was that Name, after all, who sent him to the abyss before his time.

But the minister wasn't strong enough in his faith to use the name wisely. He was mostly a mere *irritant* — like a sunburn that quickly fades away.

The minister spent the entire day there.

He anointed all the doors.

He anointed all the windows.

He anointed Blair and her father and her aunt.

He told them not to communicate with Linda, that it wasn't Linda, that it was something dark and evil — maybe even the *devil* himself, which Arba found most amusing.

Arba laughed aloud. It echoed. Everyone in the room heard it. They were all shaking and sweating and shivering at the sound of Arba's demon laugh. Blair's aunt peed in her pants and briefly passed out. Her flesh was white with fear. When she awoke a few minutes later, her brother had grabbed her and Blair and brought them in close.

"What do you want?" asked the minister holding a Bible that said *New International Version.* (Arba smiled, amused at the thought of how watered-down that version must be considering the weakness of this pastor; *the NIV must be every demon's favorite*, he thought.) The pastor was good at controlling his fear. Arba didn't like that. That meant the minister wouldn't offer much sustenance.

Arba threw around furniture and vases and TV's.

He flickered the lights.

He made the lamps shake.

He howled and screamed. His scream pierced their ears. The room dropped 15 degrees when Arba manifested himself to the minister. The rotten egg smell filled the minister's nostrils.

"This is not your wife!" said the minister to the father. "In the name of Jesus I cast you out!"

As the minister said that, Arba screamed again — this time in pain. But it was a fake scream. It hurt like hell, but this minister didn't have the faith to permanently banish Arba from the home. But, Arba wanted them to think they won. That was in every demon's playbook. The devil's minions often toyed with humans like that. The temperature in the room went back to normal as Arba left the house.

Arba watched the minister leave as he inhabited a tall tree near the property.

The minister went back home full of pride. Arba followed him. That night, and for the next two weeks, Arba left the family alone and attached himself to the minister, instead. The minister had all kinds of cracks in his home. No invitation was necessary. He had cursed objects in his house. Many were religious in nature the minister thought were of his own faith, but weren't.

Even the minister didn't know he was inviting demonic forces inside his home.

What was wrong with today's holy men?

They made it almost *too* easy.

Each night Arba tempted the minister, through dreams and by inhabiting his body, to drink and watch videos of teenage girls undressing and performing sex acts on his computer. He tempted him to call hookers and have them talk dirty to him as his wife slept beside him. Lust was this minister's weakness. And Arba used it to his advantage.

The minister resisted at first.

But eventually he gave in.

By the end of that week, Arba had the minister drinking day and night, buying drugs, calling 1-900 sex numbers, and addicted to his computer porn. His wife left him. The minister even started shouting at the TV. One time, in a drunken stupor he threw a beer at the screen, *"No, Viagra commercial, if I have an erection that lasts more than 4 hours it's not me that's going to need medical attention, SHE will…"*

It was all sex and lust and drunkenness for the minister now.

Another life ruined.

It all tasted sweet enough to Arba.

But he was getting hungry again.

There wasn't much meat left on the minister's lost soul to eat from. And when his wife left him there was no more despair. Not even guilt and shame. The minister was even starting to justify his sins to himself now.

Arba was getting hungry and bored again.

So back to Blair's family's house he went.

- 6 -

Arba went straight to his unholy work when he arrived back at the family's home.

The minister would not be able to help them. He was too caught up in his sins and vices now. Not that he was much help to the family before. He was more of a help to Arba in this case, as the family had now let their guards down. When Arba pulled this last haunting he would feast on their fear and pain and guilt for days and weeks. He would grow stronger and then plot out his next move.

Arba waited until night.

The dog was barking again.

Blair and her father felt the presence but ignored it. They hated the idea *it* might be back. It must be their imaginations, they figured. It was much easier and more comfortable to be ignorant.

Arba considered killing the dog. But the dog's barking helped feed the fear the family felt last time. And it was no doubt causing them to feel fear again. They obviously were not entirely sure they got rid of his presence as the minister had led them to believe.

Arba inhabited the father this time.

He made the father dream of his wife Linda being killed.

He showed the father the killer's face.

He again showed the father the killer doing all the evil dark things he did to his wife.

The killer kept Linda alive for days before decapitating her, torturing her, and at times mutilating her. He hated her for no reason other than she existed. Arba showed the father the killer's face. He showed the man what the killer did. He showed him the killer's grin right now as he was plotting to steal his daughter Blair.

Arba talked to the father as Linda.

"When are you going to avenge me? You were my husband! You were supposed to protect me. When are you going to protect our daughter from this monster!"

The father thought of calling the police.

"No police," Linda said. "They won't do the job right. They'll put him in jail call him insane and let him off the hook. You have to do the deed. I can show you where to go, I can show you where he is at. You must protect Blair, the twisted son of a bitch is coming for our daughter!"

The father was walking in his sleep now, following his wife. Her dress she was buried in was dirty and stained with blood. Her flesh was half rotted away.

"Take this hammer. It's the hammer he used to bludgeon me with. The blow that killed me was when he sunk it into my skull. He's over here my love, just up this hill…"

They walked up the hill in the woods.

Blair's father saw a campfire.

"There he is" Linda/Arba said whispering in his ear. Somehow she had gone from walking right in front of him to being just behind him. Her corpse lips were rotting off. Worms came out of her ears.

Blair's father took the hammer.

He walked over to the campfire.

He saw the man — Linda's killer — talking to himself.

The father rushed him.

He hit the killer as hard as he could in the skull with the hammer over and over and over. Blood and bits of brain and flesh spilled on the ground. It smelled awful.

Then, lights.

Blue and red flashing lights.

The father turned around to face the lights.

He gripped the bloody hammer handle so tight his knuckles ached.

"Drop the hammer and get on your knees and put your hands up!"

The two cops were pointing guns at him. He looked at the body at his feet. It wasn't the same guy his wife Linda showed him in his dreams. It was someone else. A man camping he'd never seen before.

"But… this isn't him! I didn't do this! I didn't do this! It wasn't me! Dear God, what have I done?!"

The cops warned him again.

Arba was feasting on the taste of Blair's father's fear and pain and anger and guilt. The random camper's body was covered in blood. Blair's father couldn't even see what was left of the camper's face. He dropped the hammer and went to his knees and was taken into custody.

Arba laughed.

His laugh manifested as a cold breeze in the woods. It had a gruesome echo to it. The two cops shuddered, muttering something about it's so *cold* for summer right now.

That took care of the minister and the father.

One down, two to go.

Arba had eaten his dinner of pain and anguish. Now it was time for *dessert*:

The daughter Blair and her aunt.

- 7 -

Arba was back to the family's house at the speed of thought – such was a demon's ability to travel to and fro in the earth.

If he'd had a flesh body instead of an immaterial demonic body, he'd have been skipping with excitement.

There was another policeman there talking to Blair's father. Blair and her aunt were crying, hearing about what Blair's father had done. They were saying that was impossible, he'd never hurt anyone, there must be some kind of mistake.

Arba waited until the two went to bed, crying themselves to sleep.

The despair and utter hopelessness was a delicious dessert indeed.

Sweet and succulent.

This time, Arba decided he would manifest himself to the aunt, and drive her to suicide, leaving Blair completely alone. He would attach himself to Blair and then feed whenever he got hungry, coming and going as he pleased.

As the lights went out and Arba sensed the two asleep he went into the aunt's room where they both were, pillows drenched in tears. Arba prepared to enter Blair's aunt's dreams, tempting her to get the shotgun out of the closet, put the trigger in her mouth, and end her misery.

But he stopped.

There was someone… *something*… else in the room already.

Arba knew what it was as soon as he saw it.

"What do you want, *wraith*," he asked the entity in the room. It was a floating torso, arms, and head, no legs, that looked like a living shadow.

The entity smiled and looked at the sleeping aunt.

She was exhausted and knocked out on drugs and alcohol. Arba sensed it was an addiction she had carried for years. Another crack. She didn't want to take care of her crazy little shit niece but she had a familial obligation to do so. But that didn't mean she had to like it. And maybe her brother had a will she could dip into?

"Lucifer's favorite still lives. Come with me. Now."

"Get out of here. I have a meal *prepped*," said Arba.

"I see that," said the wraith, as he opened his mouth wide, showing his razor sharp white teeth. "You shouldn't have gone through the trouble," it laughed as he hovered over the two females ready to feast on them.

4
ROPER

"I'm a priest, not a saint."

- Abbe Faria
The Count of Monte Cristo

- 1 -

"Now, now… don't bustle your hustles, I'm scooting, I'm a-scooting… " said the short, elderly man named Roper.

He was shouting out the window at the cars behind him waiting for him to cross the green light intersection. Roper was driving *Bullinger* — his red 1982 Ford pick-up truck with the cracked windshield that looked like it came fresh out of a junkyard. He was reading texts on his phone at the green light, holding up rush hour traffic, and squinting to see the small type on his screen. Cars honked. People yelled. And the man in the car directly behind him had just told him to get the fuck moving or he was going to bash his face in.

"Ill-tempered and hot headed is no way to go through life, my friend," Roper called back, while giving the guy a friendly wave and thumbs up. Roper let up on the clutch, which had a wooden block attached to it so his short legs could reach. As he slowly put the car in gear, the light turned yellow and was red before he was even a quarter of the way through the intersection. Roper was still reading his phone slowly rolling through the intersection, leaving the screaming man and long line of cars to wait for the next green light. Bullinger spat out dark smoke. Many of the cars' occupants left behind shouted the devil's profanity at him.

Roper never understood why everyone had to be in such a gosh durned hurry. Everyone wanted everything free, fast, and right *now*. It was all instant gratification. When he was growing up he wasn't allowed to watch TV (*"it's Satan's playground,"* his father told him). There was no Internet. And it took hours to research even the most basic of information in a library.

Today?

Everything is TV.

Celebrities are believed over experts.

And Google has made people just flat out lazy and tools of the devil's hands.

The double standard of him decrying technology while being so addicted to his smart phone he read texts while driving in heavy traffic never dawned on him.

Not this day, at least.

No, today he had a job to do and was texting his worried client he was almost there.

As The Order's leader — that 800-year old order of monster hunters descended from William of Newburg — he had a reputation to uphold.

But dang nab it if this gruesome Washington D.C. traffic wasn't holding him up!

Bullinger screeched and the burnt-out clutch grinded as it struggled to make it up the hill where his client lived. The client called him because she thought her child was possessed by the devil and didn't know where else to turn. She had found Roper's number online that morning (*maybe Google is good for something after all, praise the Lord!*) and called him. She had no choice. The police and doctors and even her church pastor thought her story nonsense. It wasn't the devil, they said. It was just a child acting out from too much sugar and not enough love. Or, perhaps there was a *pharmaceutical* solution, ma'am…

Such was the mentality of the various authorities in the Washington D.C. area, Roper often said. The country's leaders were about as smart as a used snow tire, and some of its subjects just as dumb.

But Roper wasn't judging this woman asking for his help. She was smart enough to call him, after all. And if it was a demon, she would need something a lot stronger than a man with a badge or a doctor in a white lab coat rattling a bottle of pills.

"Come on Bullinger… you can make it old boy!" Roper said as he drove to the hilltop. Bullinger sounded like it was going to die as it crept along. It had an ignition that could be started without a key. (*Don't worry Bullinger,* he once told his truck, *the only person who ever broke into you didn't even try to take you or the Bible, just the cash — men don't know* real *treasures when they see it!*) It also constantly leaked oil to the point where Roper had to always fill it — leaving unsightly oil stains everywhere he parked.

The truck sputtered and spat its way to the hilltop. There was an old home that looked like something out of a haunted house movie. Not that Roper would know what TV haunted houses looked like, since he didn't watch TV. But he'd seen enough homes tainted with darkness and demonic activity to know if it was evil at a glance.

And this home *was* evil.

Really evil.

Child possessed by a demon?

No, no, no my amiga, he thought as he touched the green rabbit's foot that hung on a chain around his neck. *The entire home is possessed. It ain't gonna be pleasant, no sir-ee-bob. Time for ol' Roper to hike up the skirt, strap on the testicles, and get the job done.*

Roper felt the familiar feeling of cold and dread that always greeted him when in a demon's presence. And the air smelled like sulfur.

- 2 -

Roper hopped out of Bullinger's cab and hit the ground gracefully, almost like an acrobat. As the sun hit his face, his glasses started to tint with the light.

Still spry at 55, he thought to himself with a grin. *Not bad you sexy old rascal, not bad at all.* He looked at himself in the rear view mirror and felt the snow white head of hair that clashed with his gray and black peppered beard. The contrast always attracted attention. It almost looked like he was wearing a white wig. "Note to self for the thousandth time: remember to have Dotty help you dye this white mess of hair," he said. "Never mind, self, that's just vanity talking. Darn it if old Solomon wasn't right about us. It's all just vanity."

Roper was wearing his usual "Texas Tuxedo" attire. He was in all denim head to foot: denim coat, with a denim shirt, with denim pants. It was what some people he knew called the "country asshole" look. Roper didn't like that description's profanity but it was accurate enough.

He opened the backseat door and grabbed his Bible under a small pile of McDonalds cheeseburger and fries wrappers. The Bible cover said, "The Companion Bible." Roper had read dozens of Bibles with commentary notes, but his favorite was always the *Companion Bible.* He liked it so much he named his truck after the scholar E.W. Bullinger who edited it. Roper's copy was dog-eared from decades of use. He bound the loose pages inside by putting a rubber band around it.

Roper walked to the house porch and felt a familiar chill up his spine.

Yeppers, this place is simply stuffed *with demons. It's like a nest,* he thought as he again fingered the green rabbit's foot hanging on a silver chain around his neck.

The door opened. A disheveled looking woman in her mid-thirties greeted him. Her eyes were puffy from crying.

"Mr. Roper?" she said. Her clothes were ripped and she had some scrapes and bruises along her arms and neck. She looked like she'd been in a fight with a cat.

"Just Roper, ma'am, *Mister* Roper is my father, he lives in a home down yonder. He's a crazy old loon, we're nothing alike." Roper glanced down the side of the hill he drove up on. His glasses started to un-tint after he left the sunlight. "I know what you've been going through Ma'am. And I want you to know this ends *today*. You have my word."

The woman started crying again as she let Roper in.

Roper noticed out the windows a farm below on the other side of the house down the hill.

"I can't take it anymore," said the woman. "He — *it* — is not my child, it's something …. *else.*" She hugged Roper and sobbed on his shoulder.

"There, now, it's going to be okay. In fact, you see those round bales of hay down there?" Roper pointed out the window at the farmland below. There were dozens of big bails of round hay stacks.

The woman looked out the window at the farm. "What…?"

"Did you know they're going to outlaw those round bails soon?"

"…"

"And do you know why?"

"…"

"It's because the cows can't get a *square* meal."

Roper smiled. He was missing a couple teeth, his beard was unnaturally darker than the wool-white hair on his head, and the woman couldn't help but burst into a tearful laugh at it all with his corny joke.

"See? I bet you feel a little better already don't you? Laughter is great for the soul. Especially when despair tries to rear its ugly head. You remember that. Now, show me the chi—"

As Roper started to say the word "child," he heard a voice yelling unintelligible words. The voice was loud, but lacked baritone — like an infant yelling if it could speak. The voice also echoed. It sounded dark and evil. There were smashing sounds coming from the kitchen. Dishes and glasses and silverware and ceramic objects were being bashed against walls.

"Hey cunt!" yelled the infant voice. "Get back in here! Feed me! Feed the *baby*!" it said, followed by its sinister echoing laugh.

The woman looked at Roper, then at the kitchen doorway. She was terrified.

"Never mind that. We will deal with him shortly," said Roper. "Who all lives here?"

"Just me and… the baby, *it*."

"No husband?"

"Not anymore."

"And the baby?"

Another loud crashing noise came from the kitchen. It sounded like an entire cabinet fell to the floor. The woman glanced at the kitchen door wiping her eyes.

"I see. Listen, I want you to go somewhere. I don't care where. This house is… *crawling* with demons. I reckon your child has several dozen in him now."

"But how…?"

"Never mind that. Trust me now and believe me later, you don't need to see what happens next."

"But my baby… he… *it*…"

"Will be fine. I'm a *surgeon* of sorts. A spiritual surgeon. I can remove the cancer without hurting the patient. You just have to trust me and go. I don't want you to see what happens next."

The woman nodded and left the house.

Roper shot her a warm smile on her way out the door. His eyes and smile said, *Just a walk in the park, no problem-o."*

He didn't want his client to worry.

The poor woman.

Her child was clearly possessed by demons. Roper knew the unclean things needed to be cast out lickety-split before they did any more damage to the child or the mother. Roper fingered the rabbit's foot hanging around his neck again as he often did when in deep thought. It was getting late and he wanted to pick his daughter Dotty up from downtown before dark. Downtown D.C. was as cramped with evil as this house was. It was just a different kind of evil. He couldn't help but think: *"For we wrestle not against flesh and blood, but against principalities, against powers, against the rulers of the darkness of this world, against spiritual wickedness in high places."*

Roper walked to the kitchen doorway.

The baby voice yelled, "Hey bitch whore — get your sugar titties in here and feed the baby. Feed the baby, cunt! Feed the fucking baby now you whore or we'll make him eat himself! Feed me. Feed Me. FEED ME! FEED ME!!! Feed the goddam baby! NOW!"

Roper kicked the kitchen door clean off the hinges.

A baby — no more than a year old, with dried blood on his legs and body, its diaper stained with shit and piss — was walking around holding a broken bar stool leg like it was a baseball bat. The leg was twice as long as the baby's body. It was hitting everything in sight with it.

When the demon-possessed child saw Roper it stopped moving and talking.

A snarl formed on its lips.

"We don't like the way you *smell*. Get out of here you old fuck!" said the demons via the baby's mouth.

Roper stared the baby dead in the eyes. "One thing about you demons I never could stomach — y'all's filthy language."

- 3 -

The baby gripped the stool leg tighter with both hands. It looked like it was going to hit a baseball pitched at him.

"We *know* of you!" said the baby. Its eyes turned bright red and glowed.

"You're darn tootin' you do," said Roper waving his Bible. "You've caused this family enough distress, you filth. By the looks of this house, you've been here a *long* time. Which of you possessed the real estate agent to lie about this place, hmm?"

"Leave now!" said the baby. "Or we'll shove this pole so far up your wrinkled ass you'll feel it hit the back of the last few teeth you have left!"

"Again with the language."

"Fuck off! Or we'll pluck out your eyes…"

"That's not what's going to happen," said Roper cutting the baby off from speaking. "No sir, not a bit nor a wit. Here's what *is* going to happen. I'm going to cast you all out of that poor child in the name of Jesus Christ Messiah before you do any more damage. I'm then going to anoint this home so you'll never be able to return. You want to know what else I'm going to do? I'm going to anoint the child and his mother, too, and introduce her to the Lord Jesus, accepting the Holy Spirit into her life, so you and your unclean filth can never bother them again. Any questions?"

The baby's snarl widened and its eyes gazed into Roper's. The baby picked up a steak knife from the floor and held it to its own neck.

"How about we give you a counter offer you old shit bag," said the baby. "We'll slice this little bastard's throat! Cast us out and then he dies."

The demons laughed. The laughs were cold and soulless, like a dozen robots all saying the exact same words with an echoing baby's voice.

"I command you in the name and authority of Jesus Christ to depart that child and this house… now!"

The baby stopped laughing. It fell to the floor convulsing and wriggling around, screaming in agony for several seconds. It puked and shit its pants and then suddenly stopped.

Roper felt the temperature in the room rise and the gnawing feeling of dread he always felt around demons leave. The sulfur smell vanished, too. He walked over to the child and picked him up. He was fast asleep and looked peaceful.

"What did you do???" came a woman's voice. The mother stood in the kitchen doorway. "I… forgot my car keys…"

"It's okay," said Roper handing the child to his mother. "He's okay. It's all going to be okay. Okay?"

"Where did they go?"

"Well, I don't rightly know, ma'am. Back when Jesus cast demons out, he sent them to the *abyss* where they would be tormented. But when flesh man casts them out? They could be miles from here or right outside. What I do know is they're not an immediate threat."

"Will they come back?"

"That depends."

"On what?"

"If you have the Holy Spirit inside you. Pleading the *blood* of Jesus can protect you from these vermin."

"What do you mean plead the blood of Jesus? I'm afraid I don't understand."

"That there is a doozy of a question. I best clarify. It depends on who you ask. Most who use that term are lukewarm believers who treat God like a magic genie in a bottle making them wealthy and healthy on demand. Me? I use the term more literally. But in your case? I'm talking about His power to redeem people — even those who're lost and, yes, plagued with demons. Pleading His blood like that makes demons curl up into a fetal position and causes 'em intolerable pain. They won't want anything to do with you. But if you don't keep your family and house and anointed, they will be back... and with other demons far worse than themselves. That's how they operate. They always come back with demons *more* wicked. They're like a pack of snarling wolves always hungry, always looking for help, and others to band with."

"Up until today I never believed in any of this."

"And look where that got you."

"Do I owe you anything? I don't have a lot of money but..."

"No, I don't do this for money. Listen. The reason this happened is because you *allowed* it. This is your fault. Let's talk about you accepting Jesus Christ as your personal savior."

Roper finished sharing the Gospel with the woman and showed her how to anoint her home and family. He then climbed back into Bullinger and fired up the engine. It shook and sputtered before running smoothly.

"It's Yahweh or the highway, Satan, you old muppet," he said aloud in his cab. "And Jesus just stole another one from you." Roper put Bullinger into gear and drove off into the night to pick his daughter up. Demons he didn't worry about so much. They were uncomplicated when all was said and done. It was the same with all the other monsters he knew existed. He had the covering of Jesus Christ and His Word as his ally.

But when it came to his daughter?

All alone in the slums of Washington D.C.?

That scared the hell out of him.

Roper drove off as the sun began to set. He didn't play with his phone when driving this time.

- 4 -

Roper found Dotty at the usual spot:

Under a Potomac River bridge feeding homeless people. She had a big heart and Roper loved that about her. But he also thought her naive. She never seemed even a bit worried about what a desperate and feening meth addict or grinning rapist could do to her. She was every father's joy but also every father's nightmare too, due to having one of those bodies men loved: Short, thin, blonde, pretty face, and unusually busty. Had Roper known what other men *really* thought when they saw her — another reason it was good he didn't watch TV — he have never let her leave the house.

"Sorry I'm late, Dotty," said Roper out Bullinger's window as he parked and shut the engine off. Bullinger backfired before shutting down — as it always did — and continued making ticking noises after the engine was off.

"It's okay, Daddy," she replied.

"Do you have that pepper spray I gave you?"

"No."

"Why not?"

"I don't need it. I told you before, my *Love* will come to protect me if anything happens."

"Oh, *him* again," said Roper as Dotty climbed into Bullinger's cab. "Funny how Mr. Lover Boy is never around when he's actually needed. Like when you're feeding homeless people in the dark, with drugs and booze and rapists afoot." Roper noticed in Bullinger's cab light that his daughter looked thinner than ever. Almost anorexic. He'd been noticing it for the past few days.

"You look more like a piece of chalk every day," said Roper examining her face.

"I feel fine. A little weak maybe. I've been fasting."

"Why?"

"God came to me in a dream last week and told me to. He said your life and Love's life depended on it. I don't know how exactly. I just know I am supposed to fast so I haven't eaten anything since."

Roper reflexively distrusted anyone who claimed to know the future or hear God talk to them. And he didn't know what startled him more: That his daughter was sometimes dreaming and having visions she said were from God… or that they, so far, always came *true*. In ancient Israel she would be killed if even one of her predictions was false. But they never were. Not once. And all this talk about some perfect guy she called "Love" made him nervous. Still, she was 18-years old and could make her own decisions. But, that didn't mean Roper had to *like* those decisions.

Roper told Dotty about the day's events as they barreled down the road — the demon-possessed baby, the family, how he thinks the family is going to be okay. But about 15 minutes into it he noticed Dotty heard what he was saying, but she wasn't listening. She just stared out the window nodding along with the conversation.

"Are you listening to me, Dotty?"

No answer.

"Dotty. Hey Dotty. Earth to Dotty, do you copy?"

She continued to stare.

"Did you say something, Daddy?"

"I've been chip-chapping away here for the last 15 minutes."

"I was praying."

"For who?"

"For you and Love, it's all I can think to do. I'm worried about you both."

Roper stifled a sigh. He was getting tired of hearing about this *Love* of hers. She'd been talking about him since she was three years old. And as much as he didn't want her to be a false prophetess, he would be willing to make an exception in this case. He had a bad feeling about this so-called "Love" and he didn't know why. "Look, I know you're fasting, but I'm hankerin' for a McDank. Not the best part of town to eat in but it's late, are you okay with that? Or will it tempt you to break your fast?"

"I'm okay with it, Daddy. Just don't kill the men with their underwear showing when they attack us inside."

Roper never got used to her predictions. But he also learned he can't alter things, either. If he tried to avoid something she said it was going to happen anyway.

He would never admit it to her, but it freaked him out every time.

And this instance was no different.

- 5 -

"Is the Colonel here?" asked Roper to the girl working the McDonalds counter. "Where's the Colonel? Colonel Sanders?"

The counter lady looked at Roper like he was nuts.

It was almost midnight, and they were in a rough part of town. It was bad enough for the counter worker when people came in drunk and high pissing on the seats, crapping on the floor, and hitting on her talking with no front teeth from doing meth. But this guy coming into McDonalds and asking where the Kentucky Fried Chicken "Colonel" is and then laughing at his own joke was as annoying in its way as all those other things.

"Sir, what can I *get* you," said the counter worker. She looked angry and like she needed a fix of something.

"Isn't the Colonel here? No Colonel? What happened to him?"

"Seriously? You're not going to drop this Colonel thing?"

"Sheesh. Sorry ma'am just thought I'd try to make you smile."

"What can I get you?"

"Okey-dokey then…"

"Daddy," said Dotty standing behind him. She was only 5'4 and he was just an inch taller. They were completely out of place in there that night where the other patrons draping the tables looked twice their size and either drunk, high, or both.

"What is it?" said Roper glancing at the door. Three thuggish looking men and an attractive woman wearing skintight clothes walked in slowly, like they owned the place. The thugs were tall, ripped with muscle, and their pants were half way down showing their boxer shorts. The woman with them pointed to an old lady sitting in a booth drinking a coffee. One of the thugs — who was the leader by his looks and mannerisms — grabbed the old lady's steaming hot coffee, drank it as if it was just room temperature, and then crumpled the cup and said, "You're in my *chair*. Move."

The old lady slowly stood up and walked away aided by a cane. The thug yelled at her to move faster or he'd smack her. Roper couldn't help but wonder what a lady like her was doing in a place like that. Where was her family? Why were they even letting her be in this part of town at this hour? Of course, it didn't dawn on him why he brought his own daughter there. Or, at least, why he didn't just go through the drive-thru.

"Yoo-hoo, Mr. Underoos…" said Roper to the thugs and the girl. They looked at him wondering who this short old man with the weird looking snow white hair and dark beard dressed in all denim was.

"Yeah, you guys. Pull your pants up. Only homos in prisons wear their pants like that. That's where the look came from, you know. To advertise their availability. Unless you fine, upstanding citizens *swing* that way…"

The three thugs and woman laughed. The thug leader said something about how the old man must be high, and then ignored him.

Roper got his food tray and walked over to them. "Hey it's me again," he said.

They looked down at him, mean, volatile, like they were about to snap his old fool's head off for interrupting their conversation.

"Get out of my face old man," said the head thug as he lifted his shirt showing a gun in his shorts under his sagging pants.

"Daddy!" hissed Dotty standing behind him.

"Okay, okay, I assume this is the guy you mentioned in the car?" he said to Dotty.

She nodded.

They sat down across the aisle from the thugs. Roper started assembling his *McDank*. He placed an entire chicken sandwich, bread included, firmly in between the two meat patties found in a double cheeseburger and stuffed his french fries in.

"Do you always have to make a scene?" asked Dotty sipping on a cup of water. She looked as pale and skinny as a couple of the drug addicted-looking people in the eating area.

"Sometimes you can't just let people treat others badly," said Roper with his mouth full. He rolled his eyes upwards as if he was in paradise eating. "If we don't say something, who will?"

Roper held his McDank up for Dotty to see. He looked like a child showing his mother a drawing he made in class. Roper opened his mouth to take another large bite when he felt a hand slap him in the back of his head. The fries fell out of the sandwich and he almost choked on the food in his mouth.

He looked behind him.

It was the thug leader.

The two other thugs stood next to him.

"Did you have something you wanted to say old man," said the thug leader.

Roper looked at his fries strewn all over the table and on the floor. He didn't have a lot of vices. But he admitted to everyone McDonalds *fries* were one of them.

Roper stood up, brushed salt and a few french fries off his pants. Without even looking at the thug, while he was brushing his pants with one hand, he thrust his other hand's pointer and middle fingers into the thug's eyes.

"What the fuck!" said the thug reeling backwards into the adjacent table, rubbing his eyes.

Before the other two thugs could react, Roper shoved his food tray into one of the other thugs' stomachs so hard it knocked the wind out of him, and grabbed the other thug by the windpipe with his thumb and forefinger, bringing the thug to his knees while choking him.

The eye-jabbed thug was yelling, tray-thug was on the floor with the wind still knocked out of him, and Roper kept hold of the other one by his windpipe, on his knees, then pushed him onto the floor, letting him breath again.

Dotty scooted as far towards the other side of the seat as she could.

"I'm going to edu-ma-cate you punks on something. You ever see the movie *Men at Work*? My favorite scene is when one of the characters — a garbage man — tries to take some fries from a crazed Vietnam vet with PTSD. The man tells the garbage man, *'there are several sacred things in this world that you don't ever mess with. One of them happens to be another man's fries.'* You punks just ruined *my* fries. And now, I see you eyeing my daughter. I want to hear you apologize. To everyone in here. Now. And then I want you to ska-daddle out and never even think of coming back in. Comprende'?"

"You crazy!" said the head thug showing his gun with one hand and rubbing his eyes with the other. With sleight-of-hand magician speed, Roper snatched the gun from the thug's pants.

"Dummy. If you're going to flash your gun, have the sense to *guard* it. See how easily I just took that? Here, try again." Roper handed the gun back to the thug. The thug's girlfriend laughed as this unassuming old man in the all-denim get-up was making fools of these three men who thought they owned the place.

The leader thug grunted, looked at the gun, racked the slide, and pointed it right at Roper again. Roper smiled. With that same sleight-of-hand magician speed, he grabbed the thug's gun hand again. This time he twisted it in a way where the thug's trigger finger broke as he disarmed him. The breaking finger made a loud snapping sound. The thug howled in pain.

"Kids," said Roper. "No common sense. Probably from watching so much TV. It's the devil's playground my friends. The devil's playground."

The three thugs backed off as Roper released the gun's magazine, emptied the chambered bullet, and put the magazine and bullets in his pocket. He then threw the gun in the garbage.

"There, now it'll be a *fair* fight. I don't want some stray bullet to hit my daughter. Are you chuckle heads ready?"

The fight didn't last more than a few seconds.

Before the thugs knew what happened, they were all on the floor from Roper handing them a beating using some kind of fighting style they'd never seen before. They were all bleeding. One had a broken arm. Another's knee was kicked in causing him so much pain he was screaming for help. And the third was struggling to breathe due to a few well-placed throat jabs.

"Why the sour puss faces?" asked Roper. "I went *easy* on you, y'know."

"Daddy we should go…" whispered Dotty into her dad's ear.

"Okey-dokey daughter Dotty," said Roper grabbing his coke and taking a drink through the straw. It was the only part of his meal that hadn't been touched during the incident.

They left the restaurant, climbed into Bullinger, and drove towards home.

- 6 -

Roper noticed his daughter crying as they merged onto Rhode Island Avenue and drove towards Mount Rainier.

"What's wrong? I didn't hurt them *that* bad. A few months in the hospital and they'll be right as rain."

"Daddy," sobbed Dotty, "I… am scared. Some of the dreams and visions I've had are not pleasant ones."

"What are they about?"

"It's about my Love. I've seen his life. Watched him grow up. Watched him become a man. I love him Daddy. I never met him and he's never met me, but I love him."

"So what's the problem? Why scared."

"He's…"

"He's what?"

"He's got a *darkness* inside him. I think that's why God is sending him to me and me to him. He needs me, needs my help, needs our help."

"Okay."

"We are going to meet him very soon."

"Good. Finally."

"No, it's not good. He's also Lucifer's favorite. And he's coming to kill you."

- 7 -

"It's him? Really? How long have you known? None of the Predators who went after him have been seen in months."

"A while now, please don't be mad, I love him and you, I don't want you to fight but he's coming to kill you. He hates you. I didn't want you to tell those Predators where he was."

"Does he kill me?"

"I don't know. But, that's not even the worst part."

"What could be worse than that?"

"He's not coming alone."

"Who's he coming with?"

"Some kind of terrible evil… following him."

"Okay, so when does he show up?"

"I don't know. Could be days or weeks. Or hours. I don't know. I just know he's coming. Daddy please don't kill him. He's lived such a terrible awful life. He has nobody. No family. No friends. He's all alone, he is scared of the dark power inside him and doesn't know what to do with it. He is scared that anyone he gets close to will die horrible deaths like his other loved ones have."

"I won't kill him Dotty. Not unless the lad gives me no choice. I've actually been helping him."

Ten minutes later Bullinger pulled into their home.

Roper called his home "The Bunker" and that's exactly what it was. The windows had bars and there was only one entrance — a thick oak door with multiple dead bolts.

It didn't look like anything had been tampered with.

Good, Roper thought.

Roper knew the boy they called Lucifer's favorite, or Azrael — the angel of death — as he called him, was an exceptionally strong Predator. Roper was there the night he was born on the slopes of the quicksand pit in Belasco, IL. He remembered the power emanating from the baby. He remembered those eyes flashing red. He remembered the baby's kicks being so powerful he put a foot through his mother's stomach during labor killing her before she said her last words that chilled Roper to his core and created a rift in The Order – with half wanting the baby to die and the other half live.

The boy was unpredictable and dangerous.

His father was especially vicious and evil and monstrous and the boy no doubt inherited some of his father's uniqueness. It was strange that, of all the Predators Roper had known, this one had the most humanity, even if he had the most blood-thirsty and vicious pedigree of them all.

Too bad the boy doesn't look like his father, Roper thought. *He'd be way too ugly for Dotty that way.*

"Well, might as well turn in, Dotty. If the boy shows up we'll simply explain the situation to him and see what's what."

"Why not explain it to me now," came a voice from the dark.

A pair of red eyes appeared and then a skinny man, barely out of his teens, stepped into the light.

"Azrael," said Roper, wondering how the boy snuck in without triggering any alarms or breaking any doors or locks.

"Love!" said Dotty running to him and hugging him. "It's you, it's *really* you!"

"How did you find us," said Roper, unfazed by the intruder.

Azriel pushed Dotty away hard enough that she tumbled to the ground. "A dead little butt-ugly predator you sent told me," he said. He looked down at Dotty. He hadn't meant to push her that hard. "Who the hell are you?"

"The woman who *loves* you!"

Dotty stood up and ran to Azriel, and said in his ear, "When you work in the office store, please be *careful* crawling around up in the binders. When you see the light, duck okay? Just duck."

"What are you talking about? What office store…"

"And when the monsters offer you the wine… don't drink it, you don't have to!"

"What wine, monsters… are you fucking retarded?"

"That's it," said Roper rolling up his denim shirt sleeves and cracking his knuckles. "Language. We have rules about *language* in The Bunker."

Roper walked over to the wall and pushed a button.

"Sorry Azrael. This is going to hurt you like the dickens. But it's for your own growth."

Azriel heard several loud air vents turn on and the air in the room start to take on a blueish tint.

"The blue pill powder?" said Azriel smiling.

"Yes…" said Roper, expecting Azriel to be on the ground, cradling his body in a fetal position by now. Many Predators had broken into The Bunker. And all regretted it.

"Doesn't work on me, dick head," said Azriel breathing the blue air in deeply while walking towards Roper. "Smells nice, almost like jasmine."

Azriel was buzzing with rage.

All he could think about was how good it would feel to rip this old bastard's head clean off from his body.

5
THE GIRL WITH THE DAGON TATOO

"Whenever people ask me why I don't have any tattoos I say to them, 'Would you put a bumper sticker on a Ferrari?'"

-Bill Murray

- 1 -

The wraith let out a wet belch after eating the family Rapha haunted with visions of UFOs and aliens.

The solid shadow figure slurped up his victim's entrails like noodles and popped their eyeballs between his ivory-white fangs like grapes. He ate their entire bodies — only spitting out a few of their bones and clothing. Then, he gave Rapha his marching orders.

The wraith told Rapha Abaddon was angered with the two demons' failure to make sure Azriel was dead. Before allowing the demons to escape the abyss he specifically warned them not to underestimate Lucifer's favorite.

This was not just *a* Predator.

It was *The* Predator.

The most powerful of them all.

The young Predator needed to die. And Abaddon was giving them one more chance to redeem themselves. The demons were to kill Azrael as soon as he's found. Even if the Predator looks dead, they are to burn the body to ashes, and scatter the ashes to the four winds.

"To give you two more of a *carrot* to do the task, whichever of you two kills the Predator will be his first in command of Abaddon's entire demon army when it escapes. The other will be tormented indefinitely. And not tormented *gentle* like you were in the abyss. You two are his favorite toys. He's already growing bored tormenting his vampire son. All the vampire does is call everyone faggots and asks if that's the *best* they can do. Takes the fun out of the torture, you know."

"Where is the Predator? I will render his being to ashes now," said Rapha.

The wraith finished chewing the rest of his food and swallowed hard.

"If I knew the answer to that question, that is where we would be, genius. We don't know. I have demons and monsters scouring the planet looking for him. But they're scared of him and what he is capable of. Finding loyalty to the mission is proving harder than we thought. But he will be found. And you and Arba must be ready. He must be destroyed. Understood?"

"Indeed I do apprehend."

- 2 -

"The master wants you to lay low," said the wraith with another wet burp. "That was kinda rude of me, wasn't it? But these humans have given me a touch of *indigestion*."

"I fail to grasp the inherent significance of the master's request," said Rapha. "Why cannot I go forth and partake of my appetites until the Predator is found?"

"Can't you just talk normal? Annoying. Anyway, the master doesn't want you calling attention to yourself and bringing other Predators around. Or getting yourself *exorcised*… which will debilitate you."

"Debilitate me? I confess I do not understand," said Rapha.

"You were never exorcised by a holy man, only sent straight to the pit by Jes—… I mean *Him*," said the wraith. You never experienced being cast out of a human, have you?"

"Indeed I have not suffered exorcism. Many holy men tried, but all failed."

"That's because you and Arba are stronger than most demons. If a flesh man casts a demon out of a flesh body it severely weakens you. It could take minutes, hours, days, or possibly even months to recover. And time is short. The master is in a hurry. I know you seek embodiment and to feast on human despair but you've had your fill as I have just had *mine*…" the wraith looked at the blood-stained carpet and his victims' clothing.

The wraith continued, "The master wants you to rest and hide until the appointed time. When we find the Predator he must die there — on the spot. No more mistakes. There are others in the world of men looking for him who will make it harder for us to kill him if they find him. They seek to use him for their own ends. Do not allow yourself to be known or seen until you're told. You had your meal, now go rest. Sleep. Go to the suitable host I have already picked, then find an object attached to that host, and inhabit it. Rest inside it. Nobody will sense your presence when you sleep. Do not indulge in your lusts. I will contact you when I find Lucifer's favorite."

"Suitable host? What host will assist me destroy the Predator?"

"Ah, that's the best part. I found you someone who worships Dagon, your angelic *father* who spawned you in life. And she lives in this very town."

Rapha smiled. He liked the sound of this. Dagon was the fallen angel worshipped as a half man, half fish god by the Philistines in ancient days. He impregnated a human woman after the great flood and he, Rapha — the Terrible One — was the child.

"As you wish," said Rapha.

The two entities departed with the wraith leading the way.

- 3 -

One year later, Rapha was awakened from his self-induced hibernation.

He spent that time resting inside a small statue of Dagon on the girl Ruby's desk. Ruby was a mentally unstable girl who was short, chubby, and wore all black, dyed her hair black, and put thick black mascara around her eyes. Her clothes were tight and revealed several rolls of fat around her sides and mid-section. She had just turned 18 a month before. And the first thing she did was get a big tattoo of "Dagon" drawn on her right arm. The tattoo covered her arm from her shoulder to her elbow and was in black and green ink. Ruby had always had a Dagon fetish. There was something about Dagon she found sexy, sensual, and powerful. This was despite the fact Dagon looked like a male mermaid and she couldn't figure out where his dick would be if he was ever to visit and fuck her. Even so, it was her greatest fantasy. And she spent a lot of time at the Fox River on Elgin's south side hoping to see her deity.

But Dagon never showed.

No matter how many drugs she did or how many animals she sacrificed (she always picked animals in heat — dogs, cats, and pets she would take from people's yards — as Dagon was the god of fertility, and she figured it'd be a nice *touch*) Dagon never showed up. Over time, she grew angry with Dagon ignoring her. And the more Dagon ignored her, the more the mentally disturbed girl wanted to be visited until her interest went from a private fetish to full-on obsession.

The incident that woke Rapha from his sleep was when Ruby walked in on her boyfriend having sex with her sworn enemy Courtney Palmer. Courtney was a thin blonde girl, with a dark tan, a generous pair of breasts, and was both popular and pretty. She was also Elgin High School's head cheerleader and prom queen. She was the exact opposite of Ruby both physically and socially. Ruby's boyfriend — the prom king, football team quarterback, and the most popular guy in the 12th grade — wasn't really her boyfriend, though. He considered Ruby to be simply a hole he dipped into when he wanted quick sex. Ruby considered them "together" and even called him by the name "Boyfriend" to stake her claim. At first "Boyfriend" thought that strange. But, he let her think that for the next few weeks as he had secret, shameful sex with her, never going anywhere in public with her, and ignoring her at school.

But Ruby didn't care.

She got a thrill out of it being a secret and thought it made the sex better. She was also turned on by how Boyfriend was one of the hottest boys in school, and that he had a penis that was so long and thick it hurt every time he penetrated her.

It only took Ruby a few sexual encounters with Boyfriend to fall in love with him. After that, he made her do every nasty and degrading thing he could think of. And to make matters worse, within a few weeks, he had already reduced her to what he called "concubine status" while he courted and, eventually, won over Courtney Palmer.

When Ruby found Courtney and Boyfriend in bed she was horrified.

Not only was Boyfriend fucking the girl who mocked and humiliated her each day in school, but he was fucking her on *her* own bed. Ruby figured Boyfriend and Courtney must have planned all along to break in while she was away with her parents out of town. Ruby came back early to surprise Boyfriend, and even bought him a new $400 PlayStation since she loved him so much. Courtney thought it would be hot and a great way to mock and humiliate the fat little whore she knew her man was smashing on the side.

Ruby flipped the light on and stared at them. Courtney and Boyfriend were fucking diagonally on the bed. Courtney's head was right next to Ruby's Dagon statuette, which Courtney also did on purpose. She wanted her smell and hairs all over the bed and next to that ugly statuette. She wanted Ruby to know someone had been there, in her bed. That's how much she hated the fat little bitch who was always fucking her man on the sneak.

"How… why…?" said Ruby, fighting back tears.

Boyfriend looked up and smiled. The thought of a threesome was hot on his mind. Courtney grinned at Ruby. It was a sly grin that said, *He's mine you fat little freaky slut! See? We're fucking in YOUR bed!*

Ruby sat on the floor and sobbed. She buried her hands in her face. Her Dagon tattoo was fully exposed with her sleeveless shirt. Boyfriend dismounted Courtney and quickly got dressed. He didn't care about Ruby but he didn't want to hurt her, either. He still wanted to keep fucking her on the side. Between the two women, he'd been able to have sex every night of the week. He didn't like the thought of that steady sexual outlet being disrupted.

Courtney laid there, naked and laughed. She enjoyed watching the fat little slut she hated so much sobbing and crying with her stupid fish-man tattoo.

Then Courtney abruptly stopped laughing.

"What the fuck was that?" she said.

"What was what?" said Boyfriend pulling his jersey on.

"That creepy tattoo on her arm… it just *winked* at me!"

- 4 -

Rapha had just been awakened by the girl Ruby's intense feelings of hatred, betrayal, humiliation, and despair. It tasted sweet. And it gave him power. The more angry and full of rage and wrath the girl who would soon be his host felt, the stronger and more powerful Rapha grew being near her.

Imagine how powerful I will be possessing her…, he mused.

As Boyfriend and Courtney left the room Ruby started breaking and smashing things.

She ripped the posters off her wall.

She used a baseball bat to break everything in sight.

Rapha watched Ruby smash the TV, the Blu-ray player, her shelf full of movies, her books, the windows, and her dresser. She was in a rage of pain and emotion and Rapha fed on it. He had never felt so strong. With this girl he would be able to *easily* kill Lucifer's favorite. The strength her possessed body would have would be greater than anything he'd ever experienced. It was seductive and addictive watching and feeling the girl's pain and rage. The wraith picked his soon-to-be-host well indeed.

Ruby smashed almost everything in her room and then looked at the Dagon statuette on her nightstand. It was the only thing left she hadn't damaged. A snarl formed on her black lipstick-covered mouth.

"You! After all I've done for you! I give you everything and you can't even let me have ONE FUCKING man of my own!? You're the god of *fertility* for fuck sakes!"

Ruby raised the bat over her head to smash the statuette.

As the bat came down it stopped. Something was preventing her from bringing the bat down to her target.

"Hey!" she said as she raised it over her head again. Her chubby face was red and her body was wheezing already from the strain. Black mascara-stained tears painted her cheeks. She brought the bat down towards the fish god statuette. Again, it stopped right before it hit.

Ruby noticed movement on her left arm with the tattoo. It was like a spider crawling on it. She dropped the bat and looked at her tattoo. Its face looked different. It was originally just a mouth with a beard with no expression. Now it was *smiling*, with creases in its forehead and cheeks. Its eyes looked menacing.

"Harkin unto me," said the tattoo as it moved its fish body and shook its trident.

Ruby felt light headed, slumped to the floor, and blacked out.

- 5 -

"Arise woman, we have much to deliberate on," said a voice with an eerie echo. Ruby thought it sounded ultra-intelligent and sexy in how it pronounced its words.

She opened her eyes and felt a wave of despair and fear. The room felt like the temperature dropped several degrees and she smelled something like the sulfur she had to work with in chemistry class last year. For a moment she assumed everything that had just happened: Her so-called boyfriend fucking her arch enemy on her own bed, smashing up her room, and her tattoo talking to her… was just a dream. But then she sat up and saw her room in shambles. There were holes in the walls. All her furniture, electronics, and other possessions were smashed to bits. Her bed was unmade. Even with the sulfur odor, her sheets still reeked of a mixture of Courtney's vagina stench and perfume, and Boyfriend's sweat and Axe body wash.

Ruby tried to ignore the feeling of terror and cold rushing through her as multiple thoughts raced across her mind. How could Boyfriend do such a thing? That Courtney bitch was evil, sure. But why would Boyfriend hurt her like that? What could she have done differently? She did everything he asked. She sucked his cock and let him blow his load in her face even though the smell and taste made her want to puke. She let him fuck her in the ass, which messed up her bowel movements for over a week. She even licked his dirty ass after football practice one day at his request, when he hadn't even showered. Boyfriend humiliated her in every way. He ignored her in public and degraded her in private. She should hate him. But all she could think was how could she get him back?

"Who… *where* are you??" Ruby asked looking around the room. She could hear the voice but it didn't sound like it was in the room. It was more like in her head. For a moment she thought of the movie *Real Genius*. Were people screwing with her like they did with the character Kent in that movie, by putting a speaker in his braces so he thought God was talking to him?

"Here," said the voice coming from her arm. "Cast your eyes downwards."

Ruby looked at her Dagon tattoo. It was breathing and moving around on her arm. Was she hallucinating? Did she take some more acid? Was she drunk?

"No, no, and no," said the voice. Whatever it was, it was reading her mind.

"Dagon?"

"You may address me as such if you desire to."

"What is this, what is going on?"

"I perceive the pain you are suffering. I know what you desire most. I feel the seething rage inside you, the hurt, the pain, the agony…." said the voice. The Dagon tattoo then breathed in deep and licked its lips. His tone sounded like he was talking about food and not Ruby's feelings. "I can give you what you desire if you give me what I desire."

"Oh really… so now, finally you want to help me. All those months of talking to you at the river, lighting candles for you, praying to you, even sacrificing my own fucking dog who I loved more than anything to you… and only *now*, after I've lost everything you want to help?"

"Affirmative."

"What can you do for me?"

"I can grant that which you want."

"What do you think I want?"

Dagon described the bargain he would make with her if she swore to help him when the time was right. His offer was she give him complete control of her body, soul, and spirit at the appointed time, in exchange for granting her sweet revenge.

Ruby agreed without hesitation.

She wanted this bad. She always had. This would be an honor for her to host Dagon. To let him *inside* her. Dagon told Ruby he couldn't make him dump the woman Courtney Palmer and fall in love with her instead. It was beyond his power. Even a fertility god can't force anyone to like someone else. But, he could do the next best thing. He could make it so if Ruby couldn't have him, nobody could.

Ruby smiled and nodded.

"Good," Rapha said via the Dagon tattoo. "Let us begin."

- 6 -

The next day *The Daily Courier*, *The Daily Herald*, and *The Northwest Herald* all ran the same front page story:

The Elgin High School Football team captain and the head cheerleader were both found dead and mutilated on the side of route 19 near the car dealerships. It was the single most horrific crime in the city's history.

The boy, Keith Raines, 18, and the girl, Courtney Palmer, also 18, were found at 5:00 am by a security guard of the Toyota dealership.

The police report revealed Raines' testicles had been removed and his tongue cut out. His eyes were gone. His hands were removed, leaving two stumps that had been cauterized and seared shut with heat. He had also been sodomized by a toilet plunger.

Palmer's face was cut and slashed in over a dozen places. Her nose was removed. And she had been given a clitorectomy. Her legs were removed below the kneecaps, and she had sustained several blows that induced a stroke before death, according to the autopsy report.

The police were baffled by the case and the precise surgical cuts. They had never even heard of anything like it.

Several people from the school were considered suspects.

The prime suspect — Ruby Reilly, 18 — who was having a secret romance with Raines and openly hated Palmer, was released after being questioned. The officer who interrogated her said she had an alibi. Although it was not mentioned in the papers, the reporters who got a quote from the officer were uneasy around him, and thought it strange his voice echoed. They also thought the room unusually cold, felt scared, and smelled something like rotten eggs.

There were no suspects without alibis and the masterful surgical nature of the crime had every talking head and department detective baffled. They almost considered bringing the feds in. But for now, they would keep it local. It was the most deranged event in Illinois history since Belasco's entire population vanished 5 years earlier.

As Ruby read the paper that morning, her parents due home the next day, she snarled.

She was still angry.

She still wanted her man back and hated that bitch Courtney for ruining everything. But this would have to do. Now, Dagon told her, it was time to help him and deliver on her promise.

"I am ready," she said to her talking Dagon tattoo. "What do I do?"

"Wait. Until I call for you. Back to slumber inside the statue I go."

- 7 -

Three months later there was another horrific news story from Elgin, Illinois.

This time, the story was about how the Reilly family, mother and father, were found dead in their home. Their bodies were stripped bare of flesh. Only scattered bones and their clothing remained. Their daughter Ruby was also missing, with no sign of her whereabouts.

While the police and authorities investigated the bizarre incident, they did not know a short, pudgy girl in all black was hitchhiking along route 20 going east. She wore big sunglasses, and a thick coat even though it was almost 95 degrees out.

A semi-truck pulled over and the driver asked where she was going.

"To Maryland," said the girl. Her voice echoed.

"I'll be going that direction for a few hundred miles, hop on in if you want," said the driver feeling uneasy. He wondered where that chilly breeze suddenly came from.

Ruby climbed in.

She had no backpack, purse, or baggage.

"Traveling light?" said the trucker, as he put the truck into gear and pulled back onto the road. He felt nervous. And what was that strange smell? As they drove, Ruby took her coat off. Her sleeveless shirt revealed her short flabby arms. Her right arm had a big tattoo of a half man-half fish holding a trident that was impaling another person with the name "Azrael" on it.

"That's one *hell* of a tattoo you got there," said the trucker.

"Oh, you have no idea," said the girl.

6
THE BLACK-EYED CHILDREN

"Once you go black, you never go back."

- Unknown

- 1 -

"Abaddon wants you to win," said the wraith with its mouth full.

Arba watched the jet black figure munch on what was left of the girl Blair and her aunt. Arba was annoyed at his meal of fear and despair and gut-wrenching horror being denied him by this wraith. He never liked wraiths and had run into more than a few when he was a giant. The wraiths had taken a particular interest in him. Probably, he always figured, it was his brutality. They liked to pick the bones clean of his kills. Or, maybe it was his unusually dedicated devotion to his father Baal — the angelic being who had sired him and who was given dominion over Canaan, and had accepted forbidden worship from the giant clans living there. Whatever the reason was, the wraiths loved following him around and picking his victims' bones clean in battle. When Arba tried fighting them, he found they had the ability to become like air at will — his blows and punches and stabs went right through their torsos. The wraiths would then materialize into solid form and strike back. Often, they would try to eat him and anything living around them. They were always hungry. And even the giants and other Nephilim monsters had to run from them, making them out to be cowards to be pitied instead of brutal warriors to be feared.

Wraiths did have one weakness though:

The Predators.

Predators had the ability to slay the wraiths — in some cases with just a *thought.* The Predators quickly became the scourge of Arba and his kind after they suddenly appeared not long after the Tower of Babel was abandoned. They hunted Nephilim like him down. Luckily there weren't that many Predators, and they would often fight themselves. It was kind of a relief to Arba the Predator Azrael was already dead when he and Rapha were set loose from the abyss. He did not know how they would kill him if he was so powerful he was set to be Lucifer's favorite.

But that was a done deal now.

The Predator was already dead when they escaped the pit. Arba and Rapha both saw him lying on the ground, not breathing, all the blood drained out of his body by Abaddon's vampire son.

So what did this wraith mean the Predator was still alive?

"What are you talking about," said Arba watching the wraith suck the marrow out of a femur bone. The wraith ate with its mouth open, loud and sloppy. "The Predator bastard is dead. I saw the body myself."

"Oh no, my dumb little demon," said the wraith. "Lucifer's favorite still lives. The body wasn't all dead."

- 2 -

"Nonsense. I saw it. The vampire had drained every last drop of that Predator's blood."

"You think that's enough to stop one of them? Especially *this* one? Idiot. You two were told to kill him. That's the only reason the master let you out of the abyss. Abaddon has told me whichever of you two kills Azrael gets to be his second in command when he returns. The other… relentless torment. He's coming back soon, you know. One way or another. Question is, which one of you will win? My money is on Rapha. He's smarter than you. But the master wants you to win. So I'm here to give you a *handicap*."

"He wants me to win?"

"Yes."

"The same Abaddon torturing me in the abyss for two thousand years? Doing unspeakable acts to me, humiliating me, and causing me constant anguish so bad having my soul devoured by fire would have been preferable?"

"Yes."

"Why?"

"Maybe it's because you aren't a pompous ass like Rapha. Whatever it is, Abaddon wants me to give you a head start. When we find Lucifer's favorite I will call for you. Be ready. Keep feeding, and growing in power. I told Rapha to sleep and wait. He is unusually strong and smart, but he is *naive*. That's how you will beat him. Keep feeding until I find you. Keep growing stronger. I can show you how to become far more powerful than Rapha will be. More powerful than any demon."

"I'm listening, wraith."

"Good boy."

"What do I do? How do I grow strong enough?"

"Children," said the Wraith tossing a bone onto the ground. "The power is in the children if you know how to harness it. But first, I am going to get you a *suitable* host."

"What kind of host?"

"A host with so much pent up wrath and anger he'll give you more power than you ever imagined. And with him you can go forth and build a demon army to easily kill the Predator. There's only one problem."

"What?"

"This one you'll have to be *invited* by. His home has no spiritual cracks in it. No cursed objects or generational curses or anyone calling for spirits to visit. So you'll need some help to be invited in."

- 3 -

The next day, 13-year old Oscar Qualman was about to kill himself by swallowing an entire jar of pain pills. But a knock at the door stopped him.

His heart was already beating fast and he was more scared than he'd ever been in his life. Killing one's self was a lot harder than it looked. But the second he heard the knock, the fear of dying was replaced by something else:

Terror.

Terror even a boy like him — who had spent every waking moment in fear of school bullies and being powerless to stop them — had never felt before.

The only thing that had come close to that feeling was when he was watching scary movies one night alone, in the dark, both his parents out of the house, stoned out of their minds God-knew-where, and he thought he heard voices whispering from the hallway shadows.

He was so scared that night.

The combination of it being night time and watching the movie about the demon tormenting a couple named Micah and Katie, as they videotaped each night's hauntings, made him so scared he couldn't even move. Every sound was something coming to kill him. He couldn't sleep for an entire week. And that night he was so scared he was all but paralyzed and could barely breathe.

That was "scary."

But when he heard the knock at the door, he felt something much worse than mere scary. This terror was so intense, he felt warm liquid running down his leg and couldn't even be bothered to care. It was so all-encompassing, and he was shaking so uncontrollably, he dropped the bottle of pills and started crying.

Were the kids who beat him up, de-pantsed him in front of the entire school, tied him up naked in the girl's locker room, and taunted him for his stuttering there? Were they coming to beat him up again? To dip his head in the toilet again? To give him a wedgy so hard his ass crack bled again? To humiliate and denigrate him in all new ways again?

The knocks kept coming.

No voices.

Just light knocks spaced a few seconds apart — which only added to their creepiness.

Although the knocking terrified Oscar he also felt strangely compelled to answer the door. He couldn't move in any other way, except to walk, slowly, urine dripping down his leg and onto the sticky floor.

The knob started turning as he got closer to the door.

It turned but didn't open.

Had Oscar been in his right state of mind, he would have noticed the door was unlocked. Whoever was turning the knob could have simply walked in by now.

"Who's… there," squeaked Oscar. He had just turned 13 and still struggled with the lingering effects of hitting puberty later in life than his peers. Even in the locker room he noticed most of the other boys had at least some hair around their dicks. But he had only sprouted one single hair so far. The boys in the locker room named the hair "Pubic" and one day, they stuck a sign on his back, without him knowing, with the words "Pubic's dad." But today, that was the least of his anxieties.

All he could think of was the door.

And the knocking.

And the knob turning.

Oscar was so terrified he thought he was going to pass out. *Good, maybe I'll fall backwards, hit my head on the floor and* die…

No.

That would be too merciful.

Nothing good ever happened to Oscar. Not in his entire life. His life was always about running away, being powerless to stop others from abusing him, and people taking away his dignity at every turn. Why would he suddenly be granted luck now?

He couldn't shake the compulsion to open the door.

To let whoever (*whatever*) was out there inside.

Oscar noticed his arm reaching for the knob as if by a force he couldn't control. The knob stopped moving like the person outside could see through the door and knew it was about to be opened. Oscar turned the knob and opened the door.

Two children stood on the stoop.

One was a boy who looked about 6 years old. The other a girl about his own age. Except for their wrinkled looking clothes, and unkempt hair, they looked like normal kids.

But their eyes were another matter.

Their eyes were all black — like marbles — with no white or color.

- 4 -

Oscar stared into those black eyes and knew death was at hand.

I don't even need to kill myself, he thought. *They'll do it for me...*

All other thoughts instantly washed out of his mind. He didn't think about his drug addicted parents whose friends sometimes burned him with their lighters just to watch him squeal whenever it amused them, while saying "don't tense so much and it'll hurt less." He didn't think of the boys in school who teased and attacked him — beating him so badly once it gave him a permanent speech impediment. Then, the school principle suspended Oscar after that for fighting and let the other boys off the hook — saying he saw Oscar start the trouble and the other kids (twice his size) — were merely defending themselves. Such were the connections their parents had and the influence they had with the booster club. Oscar's parents had nothing to say. His real father died when he was three and his mother married a drug dealer not a week later. The two were never there. Too stoned each night. And when they did come home his stepfather got drunk and called Oscar in, smacked him around, and told him to do whatever his friends asked when they came over that night.

Make yourself useful, you little pussy or I'll hide you so bad you'll never sit down again.

Even the girls in school teased and beat Oscar up. One girl kept hitting him on the head with a textbook each day in front of everyone on the bus. When he told her to stop she threatened to tell her boyfriend if he so much as talked back to her. Her boyfriend was a big, strong type who enjoyed beating on weaker kids. But Oscar was short and skinny and sickly. He was all but defenseless. He also had asthma that attacked him constantly. And his parents had only refilled his inhaler once in a while, when they wanted to visit the pharmacy to try to score some good painkillers to get high on.

Oscar was always depressed.

Always in pain.

Always scared.

He frequently had bruises on his body, walked around with a black eye most of the time, had no friends, no parents who cared, and not even an imaginary buddy.

He tried looking into getting a gun to kill all the bullies but didn't know how. He fantasized about making them all get on their knees and shooting them execution style. And then, he would spit on their corpses and string them up in the school for everyone to see. Especially the Principal. That man had let it all happen. Oscar had thoughts of slicing the Principal's throat open and bleeding him out. But he couldn't figure out how to get a gun. And, even if he could, he wouldn't be able to afford it.

His only other option?

He figured it was killing himself.

It was the only way out of this hell called life. The only way to end the pain and snuff out the rage inside his belly.

But all those thoughts were gone as he stood there, staring at the boy and the girl with the all-black eyes.

"Can we come in? Our mother is worried," said the girl. Her voice was monotone and flat, like a robot. It also echoed. Her black, doll-like eyes stared directly into Oscar's, never blinking.

Oscar was too terrified to talk.

He peed himself again.

The warm liquid trickled onto the floor.

"Just let us in to use your phone," said the girl trying to step into the doorway. She then pulled her foot back like it hit some invisible barrier.

"We're not going to hurt you," said the little boy. "Please let us use your phone. Our mom is worried."

Oscar snapped out of whatever fear-induced trance he was in.

"I c-can't," Oscar squeaked and stuttered. His puberty voice hit again. It embarrassed him. For some reason, maybe because it was a girl and he had trouble talking around girls, he felt stupid by his squeaky voice, even amidst the terror he felt.

"Please, let us in, just for a minute to call our mother," said the girl. "We can't come in unless you invite us."

"No!" said Oscar.

"You *have* to invite us!" said the girl. Her robot tone switched from polite to hostile. Her eyes looked even bigger and blacker than before.

Oscar slammed the door, crying, with his back to the door as if to keep it shut.

He could still hear the voices outside:

"We can't come in if you don't *invite* us! We can't come in if you don't *invite* us! We can't come in if you don't *invite* us!"

The two children continued pounding on the door.

Oscar covered his ears. Tears rolled down his face. His knees were pulled tight to his chest. He could still hear their hostile, echoing voices as they rapped on the door, pleading for him to open up.

"We can't come in if we're not invited."

As terrified as Oscar was, he still wanted to let them in. He was compelled to.

Then came a thought:

Maybe I should just let them in. Let them kill me. It'll be a mercy.

The idea excited Oscar.

He wanted to die, but he didn't want to be killed, not even by his own hand. Maybe they would kill him. Maybe they would put him out of his misery.

Oscar stood up and wiped the tears from his eyes.

The two black-eyed children were still rapping on the door. Oscar reached for the knob and opened it. He stared the girl in her soulless eyes.

He felt cold and thought he smelled rotten eggs.

"Ok-k-ay… come i-in," he said.

- 5 -

"Are you going to k-kill me?" said Oscar. He wasn't scared anymore. The terror had vanished. The black-eyed children didn't creep him out now.

"We're here to help you," said the girl, putting her hand on Oscar's shoulder.

"H-how?"

"Someone wants to meet you," said the boy, ignoring Oscar's question.

The door was still open and although it was a calm, sunny day, a rush of wind swept inside. It was chilly, like a winter wind, and then the door slammed shut on its own so hard the window panes shattered and broke into pieces.

Oscar stepped back.

He felt chilly again, his limbs were full of gooseflesh, and the terror returned. The smell of rotten eggs was more intense.

"Don't be afraid, no harm will come to you," said an older-sounding voice with an echo. It sounded like what Oscar thought an ogre would sound like if ogres existed.

"Pick up the glass," said the girl pointing at a big shard of the glass from the broken window pane.

Oscar obeyed.

Maybe they were going to show him how to commit suicide? Maybe that was why they were there? Maybe this is what happens to everyone who tries to kill themselves?

Oscar looked at the glass. It turned dark, like a piece of stained-glass window. Then, a face appeared on it. The face was twisted, and ugly, and evil looking — its ears were pointed, its teeth jagged and crooked, its head somewhat cone-shaped and wet-looking, with little wisps of wire-like hair protruding out. Drool dripped out of its mouth. Its tongue was forked and darted in and out like a snake's tongue. Then it spoke:

"I can help you, boy. I can remove your fear and give you vengeance. If I agree to help you, will you help me?"

"Help?"

"You're *special.* I want to help you. And in exchange for your help, I will give you what you want most."

"W-what are you?"

"My name is Arba. I can be a friend to you, the only friend you need, if you let me."

The demon Arba then proceeded to make his unholy bargain with Oscar. He told the boy how he would help extract vengeance on everyone who has wronged him in exchange for control of his body, soul, and spirit. The boy didn't have to kill himself. Arba would make it so others who crossed him would want to kill themselves instead.

It was a one-way offer, though.

There was no going *back* once he let Arba's dark spirit in.

They would be linked forever body and soul. But Arba said the black magic power he offered would make it so nobody would ever hurt him again. Oscar wouldn't want to go back to his old life or ever be without it. Arba had such wonders and mysteries to share with the boy. He could turn him into someone strong and not afraid. People would fear Oscar, instead of Oscar always fearing people.

The boy looked at the black-eyed children.

"Will I be like them?"

"Yes, but *better*. Stronger. You will lead them, and other children like them. They will listen to you and obey you. You will have power over them. Isn't that what you want… what you need more than anything. Power…"

For the first time in years Oscar smiled.

- 6 -

The next day all the Southern Illinois newspapers and TV stations were talking about the gruesome scene.

There were 13 deaths total and a child — Oscar Qualman — missing. Oscar's parents Hunter and Ali, along with four others were found brutally murdered. The stepfather and mother both were found with steak knives impaled into each eye, with the words "Arba lives" carved into their bodies on their arms, legs, stomachs, and faces. Four other men — whose names had not yet been released, but confirmed acquaintances of the parents — were found with their faces burned so badly they were unrecognizable by their surviving loved ones. Their entrails were strewn about the scene as well, and their eyes were removed, and replaced with black stones. There were drugs, needles, and bongs at the scene.

There were also several middle school student slayings.

All names were not released due to them being minors.

There was a girl found with her skull caved in by a hardbound textbook. And several boys were found killed in various ways — each one different, all found in the high school showers. The words "Arba lives" were written on the walls and mirrors and floors in their own blood.

Finally, the high school Principal was found suspended off the ground, his back impaled by a meat hook in his home. Nobody knew how the meat hook got there. His wife was questioned but said she had no memory of the night after letting a couple children inside to use the telephone.

The entire town was locked down and put on curfew.

The media called the incident "The Silent Massacre."

For the next several months, there were stories around the county of strange, black-eyed kids asking to come inside houses and vehicles. The Internet was ablaze with such stories, more and more being reported every day. One Internet report said it was "an epidemic!" but written off by authorities as urban legends.

As time went on, more children started going missing in the surrounding counties.

That year there were more children missing in the county than the entire previous decade. Nobody knew what was going on or who was responsible. One prominent pastor called for national prayers, saying there was a storm brewing, the end times were here, and it was time for sinners to make themselves right with Jesus while they still can.

\- 7 -

Fifteen months after Oscar Qualman accepted Arba's offer, a cab driver was called to a residence on a Pennsylvania estate.

The voice who called for the cab sounded young but had a strange echo to it.

The voice said he needed a ride and could the cab driver come pick him up? It would be a $50 fare, easy, *but what the hell?* thought the cabbie and made his way there. When he pulled up to the estate, he noticed the house looked like nobody had lived there in decades. Ivy grew up and around the walls. The grass was two feet tall. Everything looked broken down, and the windows were boarded up. It was almost dusk.

The cab driver assumed it was a crank caller as he pulled up to the door. That is, until the child walked to the window. He couldn't have been more than 14, and he looked familiar.

Where had the cab driver seen that face before?

Over a dozen other children also surrounded the car, in front, around the sides, and in back. How was he going to fit all these kids into the taxi? And who was supervising them?

The first boy knocked on the window.

The cabbie, not looking up from his dispatch radio, rolled it down. He felt a sudden feeling of chilly air and dread engulf him. A burning sulfur smell filled his nostrils. His heart started to race. Sweat rolled down his forehead yet the air felt chilly. His hands were so shaky he dropped the radio, with the voice on the other end still talking to him.

"Can we have a ride?" asked the teenager.

Why did the teen look so familiar?

The cab driver knew he had seen that face before but was too terrified to process it.

"I… can't, sorry," said the cab driver as he rolled up the window, put the car in drive, and started to pull away. He slammed on the breaks. Four kids were standing in front. He beeped the horn. "Go away you little assholes!" he yelled.

Now he remembered where he saw the kid:

The news.

Over a year ago.

This child went missing.

It was all over the TV.

"Sir, let us in. We can't come in unless you invite us," said the children together in unison. Their voices were monotone and echoed.

"No!" yelled the cab driver and peeled out, running over the four kids. He glanced in the rear view mirror and saw them get up as if they hadn't even been injured.

"What the…" he started to say, but something else appeared in the mirror.

It was like a solid shadow, pitch black, red glowing eyes, and long white fangs. The last thing the cab driver ever felt was a sharp, clawed hand going through his back and out his chest. The children saw the car stop and the door open. A black shadowy figure floated towards them. It had no legs — just a torso, arms, and a head. It was holding the cab driver's arm like a giant drumstick, eating it, and spitting out the clothing.

"You're back," said the leader child once known as Oscar Qualman.

"You've grown strong," said the wraith munching on the arm with its mouth full. "Good. Good, good, good. It's time. I found Lucifer's favorite. Rapha is already on the way. You better hurry if you want to beat him to the punch."

A few minutes later the kids were all on the main road outside the residence. They had their thumbs up hitchhiking. Eventually a large van pulled over. The boy Arba possessed rapped on the van window and asked if they could come inside and use his cell phone to call his mom.

"Where you kids going?" the driver asked. He felt uneasy and cold but thought that was crazy. *They're just kids. What harm can it do to make sure they're safe?*

"How much gas do you have in the car?" asked Arba through Oscar's mouth.

"Full tank, why?"

"Is it enough to get to Maryland?"

7
NIMROD'S HEIR

Cush fathered Nimrod; he was the first on earth to be a mighty man. He was a mighty hunter before the Lord. Therefore it is said, "Like Nimrod a mighty hunter before the Lord."

- God
Genesis 10:8-10

- 1 -

Azriel was defeated almost before the fight began.

He was stronger, more powerful, and faster than ever before. He could sense newfound power in his body every day he woke up. Even the blue powder that used to debilitate him had no effect. He didn't know why this was happening or how much stronger he would get in time. But what he did know was this unassuming old fart in the gay denim outfit was making him look like a pussy in front of the hot girl in the room.

Every punch Azriel threw was used against him.

Every kick was evaded and redirected back towards him.

Every wild blow was either dodged, side-stepped, or deflected — often with Azriel feeling nothing but pain.

Within seconds, one of his elbows had been dislodged, both his shoulders were dislocated, his right knee cap was bent upwards with the bone poking out of the skin, and he had multiple dislocated bones throughout his body. This, despite him having superhuman physical strength and attributes, and despite his attacker being an inch shorter and well into his 50's. And as if the pain wasn't bad enough, the old bastard handing him the beating was narrating the fight like an announcer:

"See what I just done there? I just socked your temples. Your itty bitty skull is already starting to fill up with *blood*."

"That's right, I just temporarily *blinded* you. That's called a 'Biu Jee' or 'darting fingers.' Hurts like a son of a bee sting doesn't it?"

"Well lookeeeeee at that, I just knocked your elbow out of place. You walked right into that one. Good grief Azrael, if you open the door I'm going to walk through…"

"I just hit your kidney with 120 pounds of force. I reckon you'll be urinating blood within minutes."

"I just nailed your *vagal* nerve. If you were human you'd already be dead."

And so on.

Every blow, hit, kick, and strike was narrated in detail as the old man told Azriel exactly what he did and what the effect would be. In the end, Azriel was on the ground, panting and in pain, vision blurred, his internal organs on fire, coughing and barely able to breathe. His anger flared with the pain, temporarily dampening it a bit. But eventually, he simply couldn't will his dislocated limbs and tangled spine to move, and the hot pain set in. He was in so much agony he started crying and begging for mercy.

The old man stood over Azriel and grinned. He wasn't even winded.

"Wing Chun Kung Fu was created by a girl, Azrael. To fight bigger and stronger opponents. I've found it works even better on y'all fool-hearty Predators…"

Even Rood and Fezziwig and Rawger didn't hand him this bad of a beating. They were monsters — Nephilim — with abnormal strength. But this old man? He was just human. Meat and bone. How was this possible?

Azriel grit his teeth to help manage the pain. It was so intense he started to pray to God to make him pass out.

"You done getting your britches in stitches?" said the old man.

Even with the waves of pain coursing through his arms and legs, Azriel couldn't help but think, *This is fucking embarrassing. I really need to learn how to fight…*

Azriel glanced over at the girl as his vision cleared. She looked so familiar. Where had he seen her before? She also looked nervous. But not in the way Azriel would have thought. It was more a concerned look not for herself or the old man, but for him.

She gave the old man an eager look.

"Daddy, that's him. Meet my Love. Love, meet Daddy."

"Call me Roper," said the old man. "I'd offer you a hand to help you up but you can't even move your arms yet. So why bother?"

"Daddy… quit it."

"As you wish, Dotty, as you wish."

Roper looked at Dotty, rolled his eyes, then nodded as if to say, *Okay, go tend your man, but I still don't approve.*

Dotty darted over to Azriel examining his dislocated arms and dislodged elbows. There was a bloody, gaping hole where his kneecap was poking out of the skin. His face was bruised and battered. Blood trickled out of both his eyes and ears. Yet despite all the pain, his biggest worry was what the old man said about pissing blood. His penis was the one part of his body he simply did not want to have problems with.

"Don't move, Love."

Azriel brushed her away with his eyes and nodded.

Who was this bat shit crazy girl?

And why was she calling him 'Love'?

"It's all good... I'm... just *peachy*!" Azriel said through clenched teeth. He tried to sit up, only to fall on his back again. He was in so much pain he felt like he was going to vomit.

"Dotty, best get the first aid kit and some ice," said Roper. "And the *morphine*. Lots of morphine. Quick!" The old man looked back at Azriel. "Thank you for going easy on me," he laughed.

"So what... now," said Azriel.

"What now, what?"

"You've been sending Predators to kill me for months. I'm not going to beg *again* if that's what you want."

Dotty came running in with the first aid kit and a giant syringe that looked like it'd be used for a horse. She tapped the needle to test it, and raised it high over her head like a serial killer about to plunge a knife into a victim's heart. She brought it down on Azriel's right arm. The needle broke against Azriel's supernaturally strong skin.

"Best just empty it into one of his open wounds, sweetheart," said Roper.

Dotty looked for a soft spot from the fight where Azriel had an open wound she could dump the morphine into his bloodstream. She chose the spot where Azriel's kneecap penetrated up out of his skin. Azriel tried as hard as he could not to scream but it was no use.

As Dotty pushed the plunger in, Roper said, "I didn't send them."

"Who then....?"

"Why, *you* did that all on your lonesome."

Then everything went black.

- 2 -

"Wakey wakey, eggs and bakey," said Roper with a corny chuckle.

Azriel opened his eyes. His eyelids hurt. He felt light headed and weak. He remembered hearing the old man Roper say to the girl to inject him with morphine and that Azriel had sent the Predators who had been seeking him out to kill himself. That of course made no sense. He'd never met another Predator other than his so-called granny and the crazy man-like bitch in DaBeach.

"Who are you? Where am I, what time is it, how long have I been out..." asked Azriel, still groggy. He didn't feel the intense pain from earlier. He didn't know if it was the morphine still doing its job or if his body had healed. But he couldn't help but think maybe God didn't hate him so much after all. For the moment, at least.

"You're in The Bunker, laddy-buck. You've been out like a light for three days. I kept you sedated. I didn't really intend to damage you so bad.

You just made it so *easy* on me. I need to teach you a thing or two about combat if you're going to keep going around attacking monsters."

A girl's voice — the one who called him "Love" — sounded from behind him.

"Daddy, we're all out of morphine. Do you think he's healed…?"

As if to answer her question, Azriel sat up and tried to stretch. He didn't even realize he was wearing a sling and a cast on his leg until then.

"You need to rest, Love, you're not fully healed yet."

Azriel still couldn't get over how this chick kept calling him "Love." Who the hell *was* she, anyway? Then he remembered why she looked so familiar. She was an almost dead ringer for Kerry Ditzler. Just skinnier. And her voice sounded a lot like his mom Irma Creed's voice. Not in sound, but in tone, inflection, and emotion.

"I'm wide awake and I have questions."

"All to be answered in due course," said Roper.

"No, now. What did you mean *I* sent the Predators after myself. What are you talking about?"

"Well, not literally, obviously. But you're Lucifer's favorite. You're supposed to help him conquer the world in these last days. The other Predators consider you as much of a monster as the Nephilim you all hate."

"Why me? How would they know?"

"It goes back a long time, Azrael."

"Azriel. With an 'i'."

"No, your name is *Azrael*. Don't you think I should know? I'm the one who named you."

- 3 -

"Listen up, listen good, and pay attention. I know you have a lot of questions. You were purposely kept in the dark about a lot. Pastor Shane and Finius and Gibson and I all figured it was for the best at the time. Well, not Finius. He wanted something quite different, and we even cast him out of our Order for it."

Roper was sitting in his old armchair that looked to Azriel like the one Archie Bunker sat on in the TV show *All in the Family*. Dotty was changing Azriel's bandages, while Azriel sat on the couch, vulnerable and humiliated.

"I don't know how much Pastor Shane told you. So I'm going to start from the beginning."

Azriel winced as Dotty put a new bandage on under the sling where his elbow had popped out of place.

"Sorry, Love," she said making a face like she just dropped a priceless antique.

"It's fine," said Azriel. It hurt like hell. But he didn't want to sound like a pussy in front of the girl.

"It goes all the way back to after the flood of Noah's time. The flood was a judgment on the world. There were basically no pure-blooded human beings left. The fallen angels had married the women of the world, and gave them children — Nephilim, monsters, giants, and things that go bump in the night if'n you catch my meaning. The gene pool had gotten so bad there were literally no pure humans left except Noah and his family. Took that old coot 500 years just to find a wife if that tells you anything. Everyone else was either marrying the fallen angels, had been killed by their monstrous offspring, or were half-breeds."

"Skip ahead. I already know that part."

"Ho-kay. So after the flood more angels came down to do the same. This time it was more limited and localized. My boy Bullinger thinks they were just trying to stop the seed line of Christ from being born at that point, so they went after Abraham and his descendants when they knew he was going to Canaan. Monsters and giants started roaming again. There was also a new enemy after the flood that popped up — demons. *Unclean* spirits. The theory is they are the spirits of the dead Nephilim and don't go anywhere when their bodies die. They wander the earth as disembodied beings tormenting and possessing mankind.

"Needless to say, we humans had some problems on our hands. But instead of turning to God for help, they turned to a man who was born a few generations after the flood named Nimrod. Nimrod was a great hunter. But not the kind of hunter you'd think. He wanted to conquer and rule, but couldn't very easily with all the giants and monsters roaming around. He wanted power. He thought he needed to match their ruthlessness and strength. So he did something to himself — we don't really know what, but some of us think he found a way to *merge* his DNA, his body, with other Nephilim DNA. It made him strong. Far stronger than any normal human. Made him faster, tougher, more durable. He could sense other monsters, and he had a *burning* desire to kill them. Like a mongoose naturally hating a cobra. He started hunting down these Nephilim and mankind started following him. He built a giant tower — what you know of as the Tower of Babel. Maybe his pride and power were so great he thought he could storm heaven itself. Or maybe he just wanted to prevent another flood from killing him. Either way, he was ruthless and violent and was just as much a menace to humanity as the Nephilim he hunted. He founded Babylon and all the pagan religions. He set himself up as a god amongst men, their only salvation against the giants and monsters roaming around. He also experimented on others to try to make more people like himself — who he called 'Predators' because he created them to hunt and prey on monsters. It worked. Not as much as it worked on him, though. The Predators Nimrod created had the same abilities, but not as powerful as his own. But then something even worse happened. After the monsters and giants were under control your kind started preying on humans… people… subjugating and conquering them. Nimrod also sired children. But only one of them inherited his… *abilities*. A monster in every sense of the word. And its abilities were so powerful and out of control, they threatened the world, too."

"'It's' abilities? What do you mean by 'it'?" asked Azriel.

"Did I say that? I meant 'his' abilities. Anyway, you are all mighty hunters all right. But not before the Lord — *against* the Lord. Abominations to God in every way. We believe you are directly descended from the one child Nimrod had that inherited his abilities and who acted like a monster himself. You, Azrael, are not only Lucifer's favorite, you're literally Nimrod's *heir*."

"Pastor Shane told me I was an abomination. *Unclean*. But he didn't say jack about any of this Nimrod business."

"Well, he knew all about it and wisely said nothing, we all thought it best you not know. Like it or lump it, you are descended directly from him. You are different than the other Predators like that. But you're no better than they are. Look at you. How angry and violent you are. In another era you would have set yourself up as a petty dictator king like Nimrod and most of your other ancestors did. But in your case it's worse. For some reason, Lucifer wants to use you. He's watched your bloodline for centuries. You are more powerful than other Predators. Even the blue pill substance doesn't work on you anymore. I have the house covered in it. You should be in agony. Just one of many reasons Lucifer picked you, I reckon. He picked you even before you were born. We were told this by a man who brought your mother to us when she was in the throes of labor pains. We never saw that man again after that. But there is something about you I don't fully understand — none of us do — that is even more powerful. And evil. And wicked. But you have humanity too. Something other Predators lack. We saw it when you were born. Instead of trying to kill and strangle your mother like other Predators do, you looked up at her and *smiled*. You embraced her, with love right before she died of complications that giving birth to a baby-sized killer often cause. It was the *doctor* we had that you tried to strangle and kill – poor old Dr. Romero, was murdered a few years back, God rest his soul. And even as a newborn you almost succeeded when you grabbed him by his windpipe and squeezed. At that point we had to make a decision. To kill you or somehow deal with you. We voted. All of us in the Order voted. It was the last time we were all together. And by one vote. One single vote… you were spared. It split us up. Somehow, word got out to the Predators about you being Lucifer's favorite. And we decided to hide you with the normal population. We found a suitable woman to raise you — Irma Creed, God rest her soul, too

— and you know the rest. But yes, it was you, your existence, which caused all these Predators to look for you. Had you not called attention to yourself… you probably would still be safely anonymous. It wasn't me that sent anyone to you. If anything, I told them not to. Even sent them on wild goose chases so they wouldn't find you."

"Good job with that. That butch-looking woman who told me about you obviously found me."

"That sounds like Olga. Let's just say she's got *issues.*"

"Who else knows I'm here?"

"Nobody. Don't worry, you're completely safe here. For now at least. As soon as you heal I want you gone. Far away from here. And if I ever see you again, I will finish the job I started when you broke in to my bunker. Get it?"

Dotty shot her father a stern look and shook her head.

Roper ignored her, stood up, walked to his bedroom down the hall, and slammed the door.

"I guess it's just you and me, Love," said Dotty, staring at Azriel, batting her eyes. "We need to talk."

"About what?"

"Us *leaving* here together."

- 4 -

"You're not coming with me," said Azriel.

"Inside voices, Love," whispered Dotty putting her finger up to Azriel's lips. Her touch kind of turned him on, and his cock began to stiffen. "My dad has ears like a *bat.*"

"Right," said Azriel whispering. He noticed the girl had a weird calming effect on him. He didn't feel so angry or uptight or violent in her presence. "What's with all this calling me 'love' and thinking I'm taking you somewhere? You sound psycho. And coming from me… that's *saying* something."

"Because I do love you. I know you don't love me. Not yet. But you will, I've seen it. I've watched you most of our lives."

"What the hell are you talking about?" Azriel suddenly felt embarrassed for even using the word "hell" around her. It was like he wanted to be on his best behavior. But why? She was just a chick. Why was this girl having such an effect on him? It didn't make sense.

"I saw in dreams and visions what happened to you growing up taking those awful blue pills. How the kids bullied you. How you were an outcast, lonely, and rejected. How the kids treated you. How they tried to even kill you by burying you in the woods. How the zombies raped and killed your woman and your mother. How the vampires killed your other woman. How you've wandered around, keeping yourself isolated. I've seen it, Love. But I also saw how you have saved people. Like those kids and people in Chicago about to be eaten by the were-monsters. How you saved your friends from those dogs. Saved the whole world even from the zombies and vampires. Daddy says you're capable of great evil. But I think you're also capable of great love, too. I don't think your name should be Azrael either. You're not Azrael — the angel of death. You're Azriel, God *helps* you."

"How do you know all this?" hissed Azriel. *Who the actual fuck* is *this chick?* he thought.

"I see things sometimes," she said. "Daddy says I'm like a prophetess. I don't know. I just dream and see things about people. And you and I are connected. We have been for a long time."

"Are you psychic? Can you see the future?"

"Not psychic. I can't control it. Sometimes I have... urges... like commands... to do things or dream about people. I don't know why. I don't argue with them, I do as the commands say and things work out."

Azriel looked Dotty in the eyes. She may be nutzo, he figured. But she was being honest. And hasn't he seen stranger things?

"Tell me about your dad and his so-called *Order*," he said.

- 5 -

"Oh, well they've been around for 800 years. A man named William of Newburg founded them. They set the Order up to watch and warn people and protect people from monsters throughout the centuries. But they needed help with a particularly powerful monster — the zombie. That was when they first teamed up with a Predator. This Predator used to be the poor soul who would have to pick up the heads of people who were killed at the executioner's chopping block. One day he noticed a head that was chopped off still blinking and gaping its mouth. They knew there was something going on. They found other zombies and stopped them from becoming a menace, took the main zombie's head and since then the Order and some of the Predators have worked together. But you don't like each other. Daddy says that particular Predator was one of your direct ancestors, by the way."

"What about your dad. Tell me about him."

"He grew up in the Church but went astray when he was a teenager. One day his Pastor named Alastair told him there was more to the Word of God than what he was being taught. He took my daddy under his wing, teaching him all kinds of demonic doctrines. Daddy said he would take him on long hikes at night to a clearing in the woods... and they would watch strange things happen in the night sky. They would be stoned out of their minds. Alastair taught my dad witchcraft and how to summon and bind demons. Taught him from a book called the Necronomicon… the book of the dead, which my daddy says he won't even talk or *think* about. He says it is pure evil. He became active in the freemasons and the church of Satan and had pledged himself to be possessed by demons and dark forces. He even said his last rituals would have been to violate a young boy's innocence and then he would have had some kind of spiritual *ascension* as they told him. Thank God that never happened!"

"I don't know your dad from a hole in the wall… but that doesn't seem like him at all," said Azriel.

"Oh, it's not, Love. That's what happens when you mingle with the demon world. It's all depravity. The most fallen men always start off holy with good intentions, and then get tangled up in evil and you can't even recognize them. It's a story as old as time and what happened to Lucifer himself. Daddy said he had let himself get so bound up in demons and evil he was spiritually deader than a doornail. But one day he was walking down the street and he said an old woman came up to him. He'd never met or seen her before. She simply put her hand up and said she'd pray for him. To protect him from the *demon.* And told him to call on Jesus' name when the demon came for him. She said to call out for Jesus when the two demons trap him in the basement. Then she gave him something he still wears around his neck to this day. Daddy thought nothing of it and laughed at the gift she gave him, and shoved her aside. He said he even kicked her cane out from under her.

"A few weeks later Alastair took him to an old abandoned house. He said Alastair was going to demonstrate how to summon and bind a demon. Then they would have the demon do their bidding. They could use the demon to become rich, successful, powerful, anything they wanted. Alastair drew a circle and said the demon wouldn't be able to leave that circle and to not be afraid. He said that demons feed off fear and negative energy — it's their food — and not to *nourish* the demon when it was summoned. My daddy watched as Alastair called forth an entity. He said nothing happened at first. Then, the candles blew out, the room went ice old, and he was suddenly so afraid and full of dread the hairs on his arms and legs and head started to stand up. Afterwards Daddy's hair had turned pure white. That's why his hair is the way it is, but his beard is dark and peppered."

"I was wondering why his hair looked like that," said Azriel. "What happened with the demon?"

"Daddy said it was some kind of *worm*-like creature with a twisted man's face — it had horns on its head and dripped some kind of goo from its body. He said even to this day its foul smell *lingers* in his nostrils. Its mouth opened wide, snatched Alastair up, and swallowed him whole and burped. Then it farted and smiled at Daddy as it was about to eat him, too. He called out the name of *Jesus* and the demon immediately disappeared. Daddy said he remembered the old woman somehow at that moment and that's the only reason he yelled the Name. He knew she had saved his life and there was something to this whole Jesus thing. He spent years wondering why God spared him and saw fit to warn him when he was such a hot mess of demonic activity and didn't deserve it. Why would God forgive someone so bound up in evil, who had pledged his soul and life to multiple demonic entities? Who was just one ritual way from violating an innocent child? He needed to know. He found out his heritage — he was part of the line of William of Newburg — the first monster hunter. The first *human* monster hunter, at least. He then sought out the Order and they accepted him. Since then he's spent his life helping others. Eventually, he made his way to the top of the Order and is the leader now. There really aren't very many left, just Daddy and Gibson and maybe a few others scattered around. Someone started killing them about five years ago. That's why we live in this Bunker. And why he does not spend much time with them anymore. Mostly he helps exorcise demons and gambles a lot."

"Gambles?"

"He loves to gamble! Like he told me, 'he's a scholar, not a saint."

"Funny," said Azriel. He was calm and at peace now. Dotty had that effect on him and he liked it. He could feel his bones healing faster than usual around her. He looked at Dotty and their eyes locked. He had an urge to kiss her. She looked so beautiful. But that's when he finally noticed she wasn't just thinner — she was *skinny*. Almost gangly. *The opposite of Kerry Ditzler*, he thought again. Kerry had been what he called pleasantly plump. But Dotty looked like she hadn't had a good meal in weeks. Azriel reached for her cheek and touched it. She blushed. Azriel felt her sunken cheek warm up as blood rushed to it.

"You look sick," said Azriel.

"What?" said Dotty. It wasn't what she was expecting him to say. She felt hot, and her vagina tingled.

"Your cheeks are sunk in, you look sick," he said.

"I haven't eaten in almost two weeks."

"Why not," said Azriel.

"God told me to fast."

"*God* told you that?"

"Yes, He said I needed to be ready for what's coming to kill you."

- 6 -

"Whoa, slow down, stop," said Azriel, not whispering this time. "What do you mean what's coming to kill me?"

"Keep your voice down," hissed Dotty. "That's why we need to go. *Tonight.* While Daddy is asleep. He'd never let me go with you. But he doesn't understand. They are coming for you. I don't know when. But something is coming for you. You need me."

"What kind of something? More Predators? Monsters? What?"

"I don't know."

"You saw my whole life flash before you and now you suddenly can't see anything?"

Came a deep voice from the hallway: "Afraid it doesn't work that way. Although that'd be a right handsome win for us all if it did."

It was Roper.

He was wearing a denim bathrobe that almost made Azriel want to chuckle. What was it with this dude and denim?

"You two are so loud you could wake the *dead*," said Roper. "I'm sorry, that there what I just said was an awful pun."

"You've had quite the adventures," said Azriel.

"You don't know the quarter of it. Dotty probably didn't even tell you what I saw *underneath* the streets of Salt Lake City and the Vatican during my travels. I won't even talk about that at night. Only in the day time."

"Back to whatever's coming to kill me..." said Azriel. He realized his arms and legs weren't hurting at all now.

"I don't know what it is, I just know it's coming," said Dotty. "Daddy, we need to get Azriel out of here. And I have to go with him. He needs me."

"Your request has been received, processed, and BZZZZT... denied," said Roper. "Now go to your room. I want to talk to Azrael alone."

"Daddy, please."

"You heard me. Whatever's coming can wait. You said it yourself, when you see something we can't foil or change it. So go. This isn't open for discussion."

Dotty stood up, slowly slid her hand off Azriel's shoulder, walked to her room, and closed the door. Roper looked at Azriel. If the old man hadn't handed him such a painful ass beating, Azriel would have had trouble taking him seriously in his all-denim robe.

"Now listen *Azrael*. We need to have a talk about your future. And Dotty's."

- 7 -

"Let's face it, my daughter is probably the only pretty 18-year old girl on earth who still has her *hymen* intact," said Roper. "So I want you to stay away from her. I don't want you corrupting her or exposing her to the death and destruction and pain known as Azrael Creed's life. I want you to leave now. Ska-daddle on out of here. I want you gone before I get out of the bathroom. I'm getting old and the ol' prostate ain't what it used to be so it takes me a bit longer to go. But when I get out, you're gone. Understand?"

Azriel nodded.

What was he going to do, fight Roper again?

Besides, he really did like Dotty. There was something about her that made him feel again. But it wasn't just lust like he had with Kerry Ditzler and Mina and some of the other girls he dated in Chicago. It was something else. He truly cared about Dotty. He didn't want her in danger. He didn't want her to get hurt. Something told him she'd be in danger if she was with him. Every girl he'd ever liked ended up brutally dead.

"Glad we understand each other. You should be healed by now. Healed *enough*, anyways. I'll give you some money for a bus then you go."

"Where?"

"I don't care nor do I want to know. That way if I'm ever asked I got nothing to lie about. I hate lying. I've already lied enough for you. Just get on the bus down the road and go wherever it takes you. You have a destiny beyond me and Dotty. It isn't just monsters and Predators looking for you. I reckon there are many in the *government* who would love to use you. I have no idea what their agenda is but I suggest you avoid them. Go back to living like a hermit. I will do what I can to keep Predators off your scent. Hopefully without having to lie to anyone."

"Fair enough," said Azriel, taking his arm sling off.

His arms and shoulders and dislodged elbow were all healed. He pounded his hand on the leg cast, cracking it open. He flexed and straightened his knee. It was good as new. He would miss Dotty. But he agreed with Roper. She was safer without him. He knew it and Roper knew it. Dotty probably knew it, too, but was too emotional to admit it.

Roper grabbed his wallet off a table, pulled out a wad of cash, fanned it out, and counted it.

"Here, over $300. That should get you somewhere *far*."

"Thank you."

"Don't thank me. I'm not giving this to you. I'm buying my daughter's safety with this money. Now… *git*."

As Azriel walked towards the door he felt a sudden chill in the air and a feeling of dread in his belly. Then, he heard a rap on the door just as he turned the knob.

"Don't open it!" said Roper dropping his coffee and running towards him.

But it was too late.

Azriel had already opened the door by the time Roper said "don't."

There were over a dozen children ranging from as young as 5 and 6 years old, to several others in their teens in the yard. Only one boy, who looked about 14, was standing on the stoop. All the kids on the lawn wore dirty clothes. All of their eyes were jet black. The one standing on the step smiled. That smile sent a wave of icy terror through Azriel's newly-healed bones.

The leader teenager smiled and spoke in a voice that echoed:

"We need to use your phone. Can we come in?"

8
BRAIN BRAWL

"Get out of my head, you twit."

- Batman
Spawn vs Batman

- 1 -

Azriel's internal "monster alarm" blasted at full bore.

The black-eyed child with the echoing voice wrenched on his nervous system and filled his already ill-tempered mind with rage. Azriel's desire to destroy the thing overpowered his fear. He wasn't afraid to let it inside. He *wanted* it inside.

"What are you?" asked Azriel clenching his fists so tight his knuckles cracked.

"I am Arba. I'm here to kill you, Azrael. But I can't come in to a place such as this if you don't invite me. Red tape is a bitch, you know."

"Azriel, do not let that… *thing*... in!" said Roper rushing up beside him.

"Let me in now, Lucifer's favorite. Let's fight. You can't stay inside forever. Let me in and nobody else has to be mutilated but you." The demon-possessed teen pointed to pedestrians walking along the sidewalk — including a mother pushing a stroller.

"Go away, demon," said Roper. "This threshold is anointed with the oil of God's people and in the name of Jesus Christ. Go!"

The black-eyed child spat when he heard the word "Jesus," then grinned.

"You're out of your league old man. A lot of holy men tried that trick on me, and all failed. You can't cast me out. You don't have the juice for it. Yes, we know of you. Some of my friends here have even had dealings with you. Maybe I'll pay that pretty daughter of yours a visit if you cowards are too scared to fight me."

Azriel snapped.

There was something about this thing that filled him with more seething rage than anything else he had encountered. And when it mentioned Dotty all bets were off. This thing simply had to die.

"Arba, huh?" Azriel said rubbing his right fist. "What kind of name is that?"

"Invite me in, I'll show you. Let's fight!"

"This thing is far more powerful than any other demonic force I've seen," said Roper. "Do not invite him in! Think of Dotty!"

"I *am* thinking of her," said Azriel. "And all the other people — kids — this thing has probably tortured and killed. Look at him. That's a teenage kid being possessed. We can't just let this fucker wander around."

"Hurry, Predator. Or I'll start taking these innocent people walking by. The things I can *do* to them. You can't even imagine it. Invite me in, now!" The voice sounded more hostile, which only pissed Azriel off more.

"Yes, we can," said Roper. "The planet is crawling with filth like this. This one could kill us all. Do not let him in."

Too late.

Azriel's nature was what it was and he'd already made up his mind. It was his genetic and biological imperative to hunt down, kill, and destroy Nephilim monsters. He figured that must include their evil *spirits*, too.

"You want me?" growled Azriel. "Then come on in and get me! You're invited!" He grabbed the demon-possessed teen by the collar, yanking him inside the house, and started pummeling its face as hard as he could punch.

- 2 -

As Azriel punched the black-eyed teenager's face, he noticed he was barely doing any real harm to it.

"Surely you can hit harder than that!" it said. "Even this kid I'm *possessing* is laughing at you right now!"

Azriel continued to pound on its face. Blood splattered everywhere. Its teeth were crushed and its face was a big puffy ball of bruises.

"Azriel, stop!" said Roper. "You're killing that there youth!"

Azriel held the demon-teen by his collar, stopped hitting, and looked up at Roper.

The demon was laughing.

"Shut up!" said Azriel to the demon.

The demon kept laughing and smiling.

"Azriel, you just killed that there boy!" said Roper.

"What do you mean?"

"That demon is possessing that child's body. When he leaves it, that kid will be dead."

Azriel stared at Roper for a moment, then looked down at the teen's face he'd just pummeled.

"Fuck!" he yelled.

"Thanks for the tickle," said the demon as it kicked Azriel off him into the wall. "Now I want you to meet my friends. Boys… you heard the man… he invited us all to the party. Come on IN!"

Within seconds over a dozen of the other black-eyed children piled in through the doorway. They laughed that same chalky laugh Arba did, with that chilling echo, giggling and running all over the Bunker's large living room, like puppies checking their new home out.

"Fiddlesticks!" said Roper. Even now the old man couldn't muster a decent swear word.

Azriel stood up and started rolling up his sleeves.

"Roper, I hope you got some more of those fancy fighting moves left. We're going to need them."

Azriel couldn't help but think the very thought written all over Roper's face:

Dotty stay in that bedroom!

The children attacked in perfect unison. Roper was immediately knocked unconscious by three of the superhumanly strong children. The demons knew he was the bigger danger. His spiritual scent was putrid to them. And they knew he had something inside him, a *beacon*, they hated and feared and despised all at once. They could tell by that beacon the old man knew something about casting demons out and it would be futile to try and possess him. He had a much bigger and more powerful ally — God Himself — on his side than Lucifer's so-called favorite.

They went after Azriel next.

Azriel swung and kicked and charged but was holding back.

Like Roper said, these were innocent kids inside.

Before Azriel knew it, they had him pinned to the ground. They each were stronger than Azriel was many times over, even though some were only 5 or 6 years old.

"And here I thought you'd put up more of a *fight*," said Arba. "Lucifer chose you as his favorite? How disappointing. Not going to play with you first like Rapha would. You die now — and at MY hands. I win!"

Arba wrapped his hands around Azriel's neck and squeezed. Azriel felt the life slipping out of his body as he started to suffocate.

It only takes 14 seconds to die from suffocation, dumb Azz, he thought to himself. *Killed by a kid. Not a monster, not a zombie or vampire. A little kid. Friggin' embarrassing!*

Azriel felt the hands on his neck loosen up. Then there was another voice, strange and with the same echo the other kids had.

It was a girl's voice.

Was it Dotty?

Dotty why couldn't you have stayed in your damn room!

"I think not, Arba," said the girl's voice. "You will only destroy Lucifer's favorite over my deceased corpse!"

Azriel looked up. His neck felt like it had been strung up on a noose. It wasn't Dotty. It was some pudgy looking girl with a huge tattoo on her arm of what looked like a male mermaid impaling someone with a trident. Was that his own name written on the impaled person?

"Rapha! You're too late. His life belongs to *me…*" said Arba, as he reached back down for Azriel's neck.

But Azriel wasn't there. He had slipped away, unnoticed, when the other demons' attention were focused on the tattoo girl.

"Foolish Arba, always misplacing things," said Rapha through the chubby girl's body. "You always were incompetent. In this case I suppose I should be thankful for that. So… thank you."

- 3 -

"You're no match for us," said Arba to the Rapha-possessed girl. "We are many, you are just one. And just a *girl* at that." The other black-eyed children laughed in unison as they surrounded the girl.

"Oh, I'm not alone Arba. Not even by the slightest integer. Did you think I would trust that wraith? I always knew Abaddon was hoping you would do the deed of killing Lucifer's favorite. I knew he would find some way to give you a *handicap*. It's not your fault that you're stupid and no match for my intelligence. That's why I came prepared."

"We shall see!" screamed Arba as he attacked.

Arba and the other demon-possessed children dog-piled on top of the tattooed girl's body. Their laughs were chaotic and high pitched. Even though they were possessed they couldn't hide the fact many of their voice boxes had not yet hit puberty or were still going through it.

The pile of children sat on top of Rapha. They grabbed and clawed at the girl's body, hoping to rip off her limbs and head and render her body uninhabitable by human soul or demonic spirit alike. Arba was so close to winning he wasn't going to take any chances.

Then the pile started to convulse. The black-eyed kids started falling off it, until, in an instant, they all scattered off the girl's body — slamming into furniture and the walls with the force of a mini hurricane.

"How did you do that," said Arba standing up.

"I ran into a few demon companions when entering town. They were fleeing away from the owner of this home, ironically. They were possessing a baby and the old man there cast them all out just yesterday. What do you think the calculated odds are of me running into them on the way here? Never mind, you're too stupid to do the math. You're probably too stupid to even know what 'ironically' means. I simply promised my new demon friends revenge on the old man here if they helped me kill you and, well, here we are!" Rapha laughed. His host's eyes glowed red. "You are many, Arba," continued Rapha. "But I am LEGION! All of us working together… I promised to give them a high ranking under me when I am Abaddon's first in command."

The black-eyed kids circled the chubby girl.

"So bring forth the fight, let us engage in combat!" said Rapha.

"It'll be my pleasure," said Arba as he and the other possessed children attacked.

\- 4 -

Azriel sneaked away while the two demons fought over who got to kill him. He grabbed the unconscious Roper, and made his way towards Dotty's room.

He was so glad she hadn't come out to "help."

What could this girl possibly do to help, anyway? She was weak from fasting, rail thin, and was a tad naive, as far as Azriel was concerned. He heard the demons fighting and barged into her locked door.

"Love!" she said. "You're still alive! I thought, *feared* you'd been killed. I can feel them out there. It's overwhelming. I froze up. I am sorry!"

"Don't be. We need to get out of here. Now."

"Azriel, ska-daddle on out of here," said Roper waking up. "Take my daughter in Bullinger and go. You don't even need a key to start him up."

"I'm not leaving you here. Besides I can't drive stick anyway. But I can carry you both."

"Then you best figure it out. I can barely walk, my head feels like it was jackhammered. I think I might even be bleeding *internally*. I'll just slow you down. Take her somewhere safe. Survive. Find my other kin from the Order to help with these demons. Gibson is a good man, extremely eccentric and abrasive… but he can help, you can trust him. There are still a few left like him. Take Dotty and scoot out of here. Now."

"Okay, let's go," said Azriel grabbing Dotty's hand.

"Wait!" said Dotty.

"There's no time, they'll be here any second," said Azriel reaching out with his enhanced senses. He could hear the battle dying down. There was less smashing and breaking and taunting or voices being heard.

"Daddy, I love you!" said Dotty. Tears streamed down her face.

"I love you too. Do as Azriel says. He'll know what to do. And Azriel…"

"Yeah?"

"I don't like using this kind of language but kill these fucking sons of bitches! Find a way to do it. But *kill* them!"

Azriel smiled.

That's exactly what he planned on doing.

He kicked the bedroom window in and cleared out the glass. "Come on," he said putting his arms around Dotty's thin waist to hoist her into the window. Luckily they were on the first floor.

Dotty looked Azriel in the eyes which beamed through tears.

"Ready?"

"Yes."

Azriel started to lift her up to the window when the bedroom door crashed down. Arba and Rapha — in their respective bodies — stood there, punching, kicking, and grappling each other. Arba tossed Rapha's girl body into the wall and looked at Azriel with his black eyes.

"Where do you think you two are going?"

- 5 -

"Through the window you go!" said Azriel as he hoisted Dotty with one arm and tossed her out the window onto the lawn. "Go!" he yelled, as the fat girl's fist smashed into his kidneys.

Balls, that hurt! I'm gonna be pissing blood for sure *now!* Azriel thought. These demon-possessed children were ridiculously strong. He heard the female say she had more demons inside her as there were black-eyed children.

But where were the rest of those children?

Unless all those demons poured out of their bodies and into the one body possessed by this Arba demon?

"He's mine!" said Arba tackling Rapha to the ground and punching his possessed body in the stomach and chest. Each hit made a loud nose. Azriel heard bones and rib cages shatter.

Rapha kicked Arba off him into the wall, leaving a huge crack. Arba then pounced on Rapha, grabbed his head, and twisted the girls' head around all the way so its face was on its back. Rapha's female body smiled, as blood poured out of its mouth, and then turned the head all the way around again. The sound was like listening to a metal zip tie being pulled.

"You think that'll stop me?" laughed Rapha as he used his host's body to tackle Arba into the wall right under the window Azriel had just thrown Dotty out of, blocking his escape from that exit.

Azriel kneeled down and picked up Roper, who was clenching his teeth in pain, and carried him out of the room. He hoped his theory was true that the other demons possessing the black-eyed kids were all inside Arba's host now.

He was in luck.

The children's bodies that had been inhabited were strewn around the living room. Most of them looked dead — no doubt from the demons beating on each other. Azriel figured as soon as the demons left their hosts and poured into Arba's host, the kids must have all died immediately from their wounds.

All this death. Just kids. They didn't deserve this. I'm not just going to kill these asshole demons… I'm going to make them suffer…

"Can you move at all?" Azriel said to Roper.

"Azriel, look out!" said Roper as his eyes opened wide.

Azriel felt a strong blow hit the back of his head. He spun around and another hit his face. Rapha and Arba were in the living room fighting each other and attacking him at the same time.

"Sit down Predator, I'm not *done* with you yet!" said Arba, as Rapha hit him with a chair.

"You are finished with him, he belongs to me!" said Rapha. "I shall seize custody of his body now!"

Azriel felt an icy chill run into his brain. It felt to him like a brain freeze from eating ice cream too fast. The demon was in his mind. He could feel it.

"Ho-NO you don't — !" said Arba.

Azriel felt another sensation — this one burning hot, like he was running a fever — in his head.

Both demons were now inside his mind trying to possess him.

- 6 -

As soon as Arba and Rapha left their hosts, the black-eyed teen and the chubby girl stared at him. Roper had no idea exactly how many demons were inside the two bodies. But they were mangled beyond recognition.

"Round two, you old shit bag," said the girl with the tattoo. "We're going to peel the flesh right off your face!"

Roper started talking and tried casting them out but they simply laughed.

He had never seen a case where he couldn't cast a demon out of someone using the name and authority of Jesus Christ. In fact, many times, demons knew who Roper was. They had heard of him from other demons. It was almost like they exchanged notes in their own spirit realm "chat group."

So how come these demons wouldn't come out?

Many of them he had cast out just a day earlier when they possessed an infant. Was their association with Arba and Rapha giving them some kind of extra power to resist?

Roper had been doing this for decades.

Had he lost his faith?

What happened?

These questions plagued him for several seconds until he saw Azriel grabbing his own head as if he was experiencing an excruciating headache.

What happened next was so bizarre even the two bodies swarming with demons inside them stopped to watch as Azriel started punching himself and talking to himself. But it wasn't him talking. That much was obvious. It was the two demons inside him. They were possessing him, trying to kill him, and talking to each other, fighting for dominance.

"You weakling!" said Arba's echoing voice out of Azriel's mouth. Then Rapha's voice: "You are the one who couldn't even defeat a female!" They were using Azriel's voice box but the voices were their own unique personalities, that made the hair on Roper's arms and head stand on edge.

Azriel was punching himself, and picking up furniture and hitting himself. Roper had seen many possessions and many times they did try to get their host to mutilate, burn, and in other ways harm themselves. But in this case, it's like they were trying to "one-up" each other, one preventing Azriel from hurting himself, as the other tried to get Azriel to kill himself.

Roper had never seen a possession like this before and neither had the other demons inside the room, who now turned their attention back on Roper. The mangled, black-eyed child and heavy woman with the tattoo started walking towards him. They drank in Roper's fear and growing despair. The old man was lame, couldn't move on his own, and kept fingering a dirty green rabbit's foot dangling around his neck.

"Rabbit's foot? Really?" said the chunky demon-possessed girl. "Superstition is our friend. You make this so *easy*."

"It's good luck," said Roper. "Why don't you come waddle on over closer? Let me give you a closer *peek* at it…"

Azriel was running through the house, smashing into walls, trying to impale himself with kitchen knives. As one hand would hold the knife high and come down to plunge into his heart, the other hand would grab it by the wrist, twist, and knock the knife out of his hand.

Whatever was happening, it was clear to Roper that Azriel would not last long. One or both of these demons would finish the deed. It was just a matter of time. But they seemed to be competing for who got to make the kill. It was as if there was some kind of hit put out for Azriel and they were racing to destroy him first.

Roper regained his composure and prayed to God for strength. Then he recited over and over the same words he had used countless times to cast out demons from innocent people. This time the demons in the possessed bodies quickly convulsed, puked, and writhed on the floor. Then the dozens (*or was it hundreds?*) of demons inside them who Arba and Rapha recruited left. Roper felts their presences slip away, screaming in agony as the Word's authority drove them out of The Bunker. The tattooed girl and teenage boy fell to the ground. But as for this Arba and Rapha — it didn't work on them. For some reason these two demons were immune and were still inside Azriel.

Immune to the power of the Word?

It seemed impossible.

It went against everything Roper knew.

But he couldn't deny what he was seeing.

Azriel was now trying to impale one of his own eyes with a screwdriver that had been knocked out of a kitchen drawer onto the ground, and picked up by the other demon with one of Azriel's hands, while the other tried to stop it. The Phillips head screwdriver tip was just a millimeter from Azriel's right eye. It looked like whichever demon was making it happen was about to win their unholy competition.

"Ah, ha-ha-ha-ha!" laughed Azriel.

Roper didn't know which demon was laughing. But he could tell any second now that screwdriver was going to go right into Azriel's eye and into his brain and end the Predator's life. Even a Predator couldn't live after having his brain impaled.

Then the other demon's voice laughed and Azriel's body started to convulse again.

"How about I just cause a brain *hemorrhage* in him and get it over with?"

- 7 -

Azriel lost control of his body as soon as the two demons entered his brain. He could hear them in his mind, could feel his body doing things against his own will, and was watching as his body tried to kill himself.

But he couldn't do anything about it.

It was like watching it all unfold on a TV screen.

Azriel yelled and threatened them in his mind. He told them he was going to cut off their dicks and make them eat them. But they either didn't hear him or ignored him.

And how would you do that, anyway? came a stray thought. *Demons don't actually have dicks. Think before you speak, stupid Az.*

Azriel also felt them accessing his memories. They saw his whole life unfold from his first memory onwards. Azriel never imagined he could ever feel so… *violated.* Every deed he'd done, every dirty thought he'd ever had, every insecurity he was plagued by, every word he'd ever uttered, they knew about it. Probably they would use that information to torment or manipulate him under other circumstances. But they were too busy fighting each other, vying to see which one could kill him. They were desperate — like two starving dogs fighting to kill and eat the same helpless rabbit.

And Azriel was powerless to stop it.

He wondered which one would win. Which one would land the deathblow, and how would it happen. The screwdriver was just a fraction of a millimeter away. He could now feel his brain turning to fire, as the one called Rapha was making it hemorrhage.

Then, he remembered:

The switch! Try the switch!

Azriel felt around in his brain for that "switch" he used to fend off the headaches sometimes when he was stuck on the blue pills as a child… that let him control the zombies' minds… and that let him turn vampires into bats.

Would it have any effect on these demons?

Only one way to find out...

In one last desperate shot, Azriel pushed on that strange mental switch in his brain. The pain immediately ceased and the two demons fell out of his head and onto the floor. Azriel briefly saw them in their true disembodied forms.

God, they're fugly, he thought.

The two demons were the most hideous looking things Azriel could ever imagine. They looked like gross, slimy monstrosities — like something right out of the medieval demon tales he'd read.

The two demons looked stunned, stared at each other, then dove back into Azriel's brain as quickly as they left.

The demons went even deeper into Azriel's subconscious, knowing he would try to cast them out with that mental switch again. Azriel pushed the switch but nothing happened. He had already picked up the screwdriver and was holding it to his throat, the other hand trying to stop it. Not that a screwdriver would be enough to destroy his supernaturally-enhanced body. Or could it? With these demons, with their strength, they could shove it right up into his brain, and even he couldn't survive that.

The hemorrhaging started again. And it was joined by his other organs beginning to shut down. It was just a matter of which one would do the deed. Azriel felt the life going out of him. He was starting to drown in his own blood.

Then came a girl's voice.

Familiar.

Loving.

Soothing.

It was Dotty's voice:

"In the name Yahshua Jesus Christ and by His authority come out of my Love — NOW!" commanded the voice.

The two demons screamed.

It sounded in Azriel's head like a loud piercing teakettle. He felt the two entities fall out of his head and could see them in their true forms again on the ground, writhing in pain. The other demons who Arba and Rapha had brought with them, which had been hovering just outside The Bunker, weakened from being cast out and waiting for orders — left with the speed of thought. Azriel could sense they wanted no more part of the power that just took down Arba and Rapha.

Azriel slumped to the floor.

He held his gut, which felt like something was going to burst out of it. He spat blood onto the ground.

"Dotty how did you do that?" asked Roper.

"Like Jesus said, Daddy. Some demons can only come out by prayer and *fasting.*"

9
DEVIL'S BARGAIN

"The devil you know is better than the devil you don't"

- Irish Proverb

- 1 -

"What just happened, how did she do that?" asked Azriel looking at Roper.

"There's a story in the Bible where Jesus's disciples were trying to cast out demons, but couldn't," replied Roper rubbing his leg and wincing from the pain. "Jesus said some demons could only be cast out by prayer and *fasting*. I reckon these are a couple of that kind of demon. They were competing to kill you. I've never seen anything like it."

"I can see them on the floor," said Azriel. "They're ugly bastards. They're not moving. And the other demons they brought back with them are gone."

"Time is short," said Roper. "Casting them out wounded them, but it's probably only temporary. These buggers tend to develop an attachment to those they possess. In this case, *you*, Azriel."

"At least you're saying my name right, that's a start."

"Daddy what do we do about them," said Dotty. "I can feel them. Their presence. It's cold."

"I have a doozy of an idea about that," said Roper. "I've anointed the entire house, every door and window and crevice. There are no cracks to slip in through. They had to be invited. I'm not even sure how the one that rode along with the tattooed girl entered. Maybe once one is invited they all are. Another pickle for another day I reckon. But I'm wondering if what keeps them out could also keep them *in*."

"Could?" asked Azriel.

"I've never given it a go before, but it seems logical. What can I say? I'm spinning this yarn as we go just the same as you."

"So what do we do?"

"*We* don't do anything. You are vulnerable. No trace of the Holy Ghost inside you. You don't believe in God as you should."

"I believe in him. I just think he hates me... being, you know, an *abomination* and all, as you guys keep telling me."

"Well, nothing is impossible for God. If He can save me He can save anyone. We can discuss this later. For now, I want you to ska-daddle. All we flesh humans can do is cast them out. Only Jesus could command them into the abyss. But there still might be a way to get them there. Pastor Shane might have known some ways. I learned much of what I know about this from him. I could sure use his help right about now. You two go. Take my daughter, Azriel, and protect her. Go to Belasco. See if Pastor Shane had anything. His church is sacred holy ground. It's been there since before that entire state was in existence. Built by some of my predecessors in the middle of the then wild forest. Which always seemed strange to me."

"You mentioned the abyss," said Azriel.

"I sure did."

"There's something you should know about Belasco before we leave."

- 2 -

"Well, that fills in some gaps in my education," said Roper after Azriel told him about the fight with Fezziwig, and the door to the abyss in Belasco. "We always knew there was something rotten about that town. Something evil. Something there probing people, and influencing them. But we had no idea there was a doorway to the abyss. No idea just *how* evil that place is."

"That's not all," said Azriel.

"What do you mean."

"Finius and I made a pact. Someone needed to stay in Belasco and watch over it. I left, he stayed. I don't trust him. But maybe, just maybe… he has some ideas on how to banish these things," Azriel looked at the ground. The two wounded demons were still out cold. Their grotesque faces twitched as if they were both having a nightmare.

"I don't want my daughter here. Like it or lump it we need Finius's help. Maybe he knows something. Hurry. Go. For all we know these filthy jackanapes will attack any minute. I need time to re-anoint the house."

"I want us to stay together, all three of us," said Dotty. "If they attack again how will you stop them?"

"I don't have the foggiest idea. But at least you're safe."

"Daddy, I — "

"Enough. Your father has spoken. Go with Azriel to Belasco. Help him if you can. Don't worry about a thing. Just make like a tree and *leave*. Now."

Azriel grabbed Dotty's hand, "Let's go," he said, and yanked her out the house.

As Roper watched them leave he couldn't ignore the growing pit in his stomach telling him something bad was going to happen.

Something *really* bad.

Not just something bad to him, but to his only daughter, too.

- 3 -

Roper immediately went to the kitchen and grabbed a flask from the cupboard marked "OIL" on it. He limped around, his foot and leg felt like they were fractured in multiple areas (*deal with that later, ignore the pain, keep moving*… he told himself over and over). He went to all the doors and windows, and one-by-one put some oil on the inside and outside of each, and anointed them.

He felt a strong sense of urgency.

He didn't know if the demons were awake yet or not. But he couldn't shake the feeling that something was watching him, smiling and laughing and letting him think he was "winning" just waiting for the right time to attack and kill him. Roper knew the enemy's way was to let people think they had power. Often times, it was power over them, power that they could bind and control and summon them. But what always happened… what happened to his old mentor Alastair… was the demons toyed with humans, instead. It amused the demons to let man have a small victory here, or a little accomplishment there. Then, when that man wasn't expecting it — destroy his life. That was the way demons operated. And Roper couldn't shake the feeling that was happening to him now. These demons were especially powerful – of that same class as the ones Jesus said could only be cast out by prayer and fasting.

No wonder his daughter had stopped eating and always looked like she was spaced out, but was really constantly praying. How did Roper not remember that story? He was ashamed for being so rusty on his Book of Mark.

Dotty was always having visions and feelings. She could never explain them, she just went with them — submissive and obedient. Roper knew she was way too good for Azriel, who was undisciplined, impatient, and too prone to act without thinking. *A fire-ready-aim kind of guy*. He was going to get himself killed eventually. It was inevitable, as far as Roper was concerned. He was amazed it hadn't already happened. But if there was one thing this Azriel kid had… it was luck.

But luck always runs out. And when it does, it's never pretty, Roper thought.

When Roper finished anointing the house in the last room — the loft upper floor where he had nothing but a few trunks and his wooden Kung Fu practice dummy — he realized he was almost out of oil. *Thank God I had just enough,* he thought as he felt the dirty green rabbit's foot around his neck again. He knew if people understood that rabbit's foot, he'd be a mark not just for demonic forces, but monsters, and even humans in-the-know who would understand and try to destroy (or misuse it) it.

It was like a nuclear bomb.

And, like any nuclear bomb, you don't use it unless absolutely necessary.

As Roper walked down the stairs, a cold rush of air penetrated his bones. It was the same feeling he experienced whenever he was in the presence of demons. But this was especially chilling. Like what he felt when Azriel let the black-eyed teen into the house.

Were the demons awake?

Were they waiting for him downstairs in the living room?

He imagined them waiting for him, grins on their invisible faces, ready to torment him the second he opened the door to leave. Or, even worse, allow him to leave, then follow him outside — just to let him think he'd won — and then corner him and tear him apart piece by piece.

"Don't be a chicken," he said aloud to himself. "We have God on our side. How can we lose?"

Roper limped down the attic stairs.

One step.

Then another.

Then another.

Every sound he heard in the house, every creak of the steps, every knock of a pipe, he assumed the sound was from demons messing with him. When he made it to the bottom of the stairs he looked at the living room floor. It was a chaotic mess. Several dead children were strewn about the room like dirty clothes that had missed the hamper. *How in the world am I going to explain this to the authorities?* He stared right at the spot where Azriel said the two demons were lying. His heart was pounding fast. He could feel the blood pumping through his pulses in his wrist, neck, and fingers.

What's the matter with you, you old 'fraidy cat! You've walked through houses infested with far more demons than this! he thought.

Then, a counter thought:

Yeah, well, them demons weren't this kind of demons.

I may be scared, but I can still act… he thought. *Yes, I can still act!*

Roper tried to run, but his leg gave out and he fell on the floor face down.

Drats! he thought.

He got back up and limped to the door as fast as he could, trying to ignore his leg pain.

He imagined the demons standing over him. He was only a few feet from the door now. Just two more steps…

He reached the door.

He tried to turn the knob.

Locked! They're on to me!

No, he remembered.

He locked the door behind him after anointing the outside of it — a habit from childhood.

He unlocked the door.

It was slippery from the oil on his hands.

He opened the door and felt a rush of cold air hit him. But it wasn't coming from the outside of the house. It was coming from the inside. They were coming for him. He could feel it. He grit his teeth and dove over the stoop onto the walkway.

The door was still open.

He didn't think it mattered, but in one last movement he pushed it shut.

The moment it shut he heard a loud thump hit the other side as something ran into it.

Roper had escaped by a mere fraction of a second.

I just hope this idea works, and they can't leave, he thought as he limped over to Bullinger, which was still parked in the driveway. He was irritated Azriel and Dotty didn't take the truck as he instructed. But as his leg throbbed he was also glad for the ride.

- 4 -

Arba and Rapha felt groggy and weak when they regained consciousness. For a split second they both thought they were still flesh giants back in the day, awakening on a battlefield.

But they weren't back in the old days.

They were in a house.

On a floor.

And, in a great deal of pain.

What did that girl do to them? How did she have the authority to do what she did? They heard the abominable name "Jesus" and "come out." The next thing they felt was a surge of pain running up and through their disembodied beings. Then blackness. Until awakening just now.

They got up and looked at each other.

They were still too weak and in too much pain to fight, although the thought did cross their minds for a moment.

"Where are they?" they both said at the same time.

They looked around the living room, still unable to move, admiring the chaos they caused — the broken furniture and appliances, the dead children strewn about the floor, whose bodies were beaten and bloodied from the fight with Lucifer's favorite and each other.

"They have clearly vacated the premises," said Rapha.

"Wrong, genius. There is still someone inside, hear that?"

There was a sound coming from upstairs, and walking down the steps.

"It's the old man!" said Arba. "His ass is mine!"

Arba tried to get up but slumped back down. He was still too weak. Rapha tried the same, and met the same result.

They watched the old man limp down the stairs, concentrating all their will on moving, to see which one could take him first and tear him apart.

But neither could move. With every passing moment they felt strength returning, their power coming back. As the old man limped past them, Rapha tried to grab onto his ankle, but his hand went right through him. He still wasn't able to manifest himself physically yet. The old man couldn't hear them talking, either, it seemed. But Rapha could feel that ability to materialize coming back.

As the old man reached the door both the demons could now move and manifest themselves physically. They couldn't possess the old man but they could feast on his terror. The fear he was experiencing now was especially tasty. They both wanted more. A holy man — a true holy man — in terror is a meal neither had ever tasted before. They rushed the door as fast as they could. But as they made it to the open doorway just inches away from the old man, they were knocked back by an invisible barrier.

They both fell back to the ground.

As the old man pushed the door closed they rushed him again. This time hitting the barrier and the door at the same time.

"Dammit!" said Arba.

"He's bound us here. We can't leave. This does not bode well, not at all," said Rapha.

"No shit, Sherlock."

The two demons spent the rest of the day searching the house for a way out. But every window and door, and even the fireplace had that strange barrier up that wouldn't let them leave.

They were trapped.

And, for all they knew, they'd be there forever, suffering each other's company. Abyss version 2.0.

"This is unacceptable," said Rapha, noticing the sun setting.

"Being stuck with you with not even a deck of cards to pass time is worse than the abyss," said Arba.

The two demons snarled and attacked each other. And why not? What else was there to do but fight? If one could somehow kill the other — if that was even possible — then the one could wait for an opportunity to escape and still complete the mission.

They fought through the house. They threw knives at each other, they threw furniture at each other, they punched each other and attacked each other. But they had no lasting effect on each other and eventually stopped.

As the moon appeared they felt something they hadn't felt since the moment when their consciousness awoke in the abyss after Jesus Himself cast them there:

Despair.

They both howled and screamed.

The noise was so loud and high-pitched dogs and other stray animals around the entire neighborhood quivered and hid. Every man, woman, and child in the neighborhood felt a cold rush of terror sweep through their bodies.

Then, the front door opened slowly.

They both rushed down the stairs.

Did the old fool come back?

Oh good!

No, it wasn't the old man.

They saw the wraith dragging a naked man, bound and gagged, behind him through the threshold.

"I cannot believe Abaddon has put his faith in you two nitwits," said the wraith. His legless body floated inside. He threw the bound man to the ground.

"You!" said Rapha and Arba simultaneously.

"Yes, me," said the wraith licking his snow-white fangs.

"Have you come to free us?" said Arba.

"I've come to warn you," said the wraith. "Abaddon is pissed. When I told him you were stuck inside here, outwitted by a human girl, he said to leave you in here. Stuck and bound until he escaped and could deal with you himself. But personally, I like you two. So I went to *bat* for you."

"Let us out of here!" said Arba.

"Yes, grant us escape!"

"Why? So you two can fail again and make more messes? So you can just fight each other again and get bitch slapped by a skinny little whore? Why should I?"

"I'll rip them apart," said Arba.

"No, I will be the one to deal the striking blow," said Rapha.

"You'll do it over my dead disembodied soul!" said Arba shoving Rapha aside. Rapha shoved him back.

"Enough!" yelled the wraith. "My ass is as much on the line as yours now. I vouched for you. That means if you fail, I fail. If I fail, I'm as doomed as you. Got it?"

Arba and Rapha nodded.

"Good. Now sit down, shut up, and listen to my plan. I know a way you can kill all three of them. And this time, I'm going to help you, to make sure the job is done right."

- 5 -

"Which of us are you going to help?" asked Arba.

"Yes, are you going to assist my noble self, or this dung pile?" said Rapha.

"Piss off," said Arba.

"You two are like a couple of little girls. Shut the hell up. I'm going to help you both."

"But only one of us can be freed of perdition," said Rapha. "Only one of us can win."

"Well, see, that's where you two jackasses are wrong," said the wraith. "I made a suggestion to Abaddon that if you work together, if your fates are intertwined, that you would be more likely to kill Lucifer's favorite. There are no other demons more powerful than you on the planet. Being direct children of Dagon and Baal, your spirits are stronger than other demons. Abaddon was wanting it to be one of you. But why not both? In life you warred with each other and look where that got you? Then later, cast into the abyss at the same time, tormented together. You can do it differently. You can avoid the same mistakes. Or you can fail. But now you have an incentive to help each other. If you win, you will both be Abaddon's first in command under his favorite. If you lose, back to the abyss you both go. Teamwork, boys, teamwork."

"How can we be sent back?"

"Idiot. You think Abaddon would have let you out if he didn't know how to get you back in? If I were you I would work together, boys. Azrael is growing more powerful by the day. Eventually he will learn how to wield his power. You best kill him now, for all our sakes. So swear an oath to help each other."

"A devil's bargain?" said Rapha. "I accept. What about you, Arba? Why not join forces for mutual survival and triumph?"

"Awright," said Arba. "But this doesn't mean I have to *like* you."

"I concur."

"Good," said the wraith. "Now that you've kissed and made up, here is the plan…"

- 6 -

"Obviously, you two are vulnerable to the girl," said the wraith. "She knows the rules. She understands how to cast you out. So just possessing someone and going after them again will be another failure."

"What solution to this dilemma do you propose?" asked Rapha.

"There is a *loophole.* This is unprecedented. Realize there haven't been demons as powerful as you since Jesus walked the earth." The wraith made a face, as if he wanted to spit, when he said "Jesus."

"What are you talking about," said Arba.

"What I'm saying is, no demon has ever tried to possess a non-human. But if you did, you wouldn't be able to be cast out."

"You mean possess animals? That won't make us powerful enough. Surely you jest," said Rapha.

"No not animals. Non-humans. Other Nephilim. And *Predators*."

"How do you know this?"

"I don't, for sure. But there is no record of Jesus helping Nephilim kind before. Nor did He help any of the Predators. Both Nephilim and Predators are abominations. We can use that to our advantage. There is one catch, though."

"What catch?" asked the two demons simultaneously.

There was always a catch.

Always.

"You will need their *permission*. A Nephilim spirit is already a demon, it's just embodied in its own skin it was born with. A Predator by instinct will want to destroy you. But they have Nephilim attributes. I believe it's possible. But you would need their permission."

"What monster and what Predator would give us that kind of access?" asked Rapha.

"You two really are stupid, you know that?" said the wraith. "Think about it. Lucifer's favorite has no doubt made many enemies. Did you try to inhabit him?"

"Yes, he somehow cast us out. But we were able to get back in. It was only temporary."

"Did you read his mind?"

"We have instant access to anyone's memories we possess."

"Keep going…" said the wraith.

"And… he *does* have enemies. Mortal enemies who would die for the ability to take his life!" said Rapha.

"There were two in particular who hated him who are still alive. Three if you count the zombie," said Arba.

"Don't bother with anything zombie," said the wraith. "Nor the vampires — those are Abaddon's personal children from his seed. Even if there were any vampires around you'd be forbidden."

"There are two who hate Lucifer's favorite we could possess," said Rapha looking at Arba who nodded in agreement.

"Good," said the wraith. "Agree on who goes after which, and then let's get you out of here."

"How will you do that? We are bound by anointing."

The wraith pointed towards the naked man on the floor. He was sobbing, but they hadn't noticed the whole time.

"That's what *he's* for," said the wraith licking his chops.

- 7 -

"Get up!" said the wraith to the naked man after loosening his binds.

The man was terrified. In the presence of two demons and this floating shadow with the long fangs, he thought he was in hell or worse. One minute he was walking to his car leaving the funeral home he worked at for the night. The next he was hit over the head. He awoke to being dragged along the sidewalk. His blood from his scraped back and legs left a trail. He tried to move but the shadow's grip was like a vice. It turned to look at him, declaring, "Do as I say and this will all be over with quickly, understand?" The man nodded. "You'll be *with* your family before the night is over, I promise," said the shadow.

Then, the man was tossed inside this house. He was shaking and shivering in terror the whole time watching the shadow man talking to himself. It didn't dawn on him until a few minutes in that the shadow was talking to two invisible things.

"How can he help us escape here?" asked Arba.

"Watch and learn, you idiots," said the wraith turning to the naked man. "What's your name?"

"Joe…"

"Okay Joe, I told you that you'd be *with* your family before the night is over, right? I am a wraith of my word. Relax. Step outside the front door."

The man named Joe started walking towards the door but then was stopped by the wraith's voice.

"Joe, just know if you try to run I WILL catch you. And I will kill you where you stand. And then kill your family — slow and painful-like. Get it?"

Joe nodded and walked outside the door.

He was too scared to talk but looked at the wraith as if saying, "Now what?"

"I want you to say the following and I want you to *mean* it. And Joe, I'll know if you don't mean it. And I will cut your balls off, then your arms, then your legs, and watch you bleed out to death. Got it?"

Joe nodded. He looked like he was about to faint.

"Say these words… 'Arba and Rapha I invite you to cross this threshold.'"

Joe opened his mouth to talk but was too scared.

"Do it!" yelled the wraith.

"Arba and R-Rapha… I invite you to cross this threshold…"

Arba and Rapha raced towards the door. The barrier was gone. The wraith's theory had worked.

"Good boy, Joe" said the wraith. "Now come here."

The man walked back through the door. Rapha and Arba pushed him in towards the wraith. A bit of fun to kick the night off.

"I am going to eat you now. For your obedience, I will kill you first, so you won't have to watch me slurp up your tasty entrails."

"But you said… I would be with my family…"

"And you will, Joe. I promise to eat *them* next. You'll all be inside me together. I told you I am a wraith of my word."

The wraith opened his mouth wide and swallowed the man's head, chewing it off and gulping it down. The naked headless body twitched and then slumped to the ground.

"Okay you two, you have your marching orders," said the wraith with his mouth full crunching on the skull and swallowing. "Do you know who's going for which host?"

The two demons nodded.

"Good. Hurry. Get your hosts, and then go immediately to the town called Belasco where you escaped the abyss. They'll be there, and they won't have any idea of what's coming. Now leave me, I like to eat alone."

The wraith closed the front door.

"Joe, huh? I do so love eating *sloppy Joe's…*" it said as he slurped up Joe's entrails.

10
MONSTER TOWN

"Sometimes human places create inhuman monsters."

- Stephen King
The Shining

- 1 -

"You said you have dreams and visions," said Azriel, as he and Dotty walked along the back Indiana road towards the Illinois border. It'd been three days since leaving Maryland and they'd decided to avoid people. When demons were involved, they could be anywhere, possessing anyone, and why take chances?

"I do, Love. Although since the demon fight they seemed to have stopped."

"Tell me about them."

"They are mostly just… feelings… I get. Not necessarily clear images although some are. Like God is putting something in my heart. Often I can't even put words to what I'm feeling, so I just *submit* to them. Usually I forget about them just like forgetting a dream."

"Do you remember what you said to me before about an office store and monsters offering me wine?"

"I remember saying it, I don't remember the dreams vividly though. Sorry. Sometimes in cases like that I just get the image or feeling and then it passes."

"Well, I'm not so lucky."

"What do you mean, Love?"

"I have them too. Sort of. Sometimes. I think. *Hellz*… I don't know. But the last couple months I keep have a recurring dream. Someone's dying a bloody, violent, painful death."

"That's awful!"

"Yeah. I sometimes see someone… I can't tell who it is. I think it's me. The person, me, whoever… is burning to death in a giant furnace. Invisible things, *entities*, I don't know what they are… are laughing and cheering it on. Once I had this vision so clearly I drew it on paper. After what's happened I think it might be these demons."

"It might be or it might not. With visions you can't alter it. They just happen. I wish there was some way to contact Daddy, I'm worried. The look in his eyes when we left… nah-boo."

"Nah-boo?"

"Just an expression we use sometimes."

Azriel found himself genuinely liking this girl despite her corniness. Unlike all the girls he had dated when he lived in Chicago, this girl wasn't damaged. She didn't seem to have hang-ups about stupid irrelevant things or pined after an ex-boyfriend. She was submissive, and sweet, and nice, and kind, and agreeable, and nurturing. She was the exact opposite of all the girls he'd met in his almost 21-year lifespan.

Your dad was right, Azriel thought, *you probably are the last hot girl on earth, same age as me, with your hymen still intact.*

They saw streetlights ahead.

It was Radu Falls — one of the many small, forgotten Illinois towns on the Indiana border. It was also the only town in the area with a bus stop. Azriel had used it twice before. The bench still had an ad for a slick looking lawyer named Max Sydow. Max was apparently an older man, one who looked more like a priest than a lawyer going by his picture. Maybe that was part of his marketing plan, Azriel wondered. That advertising copywriter part of him spoke up: *You can take the boy out of the advertising business, but you can't take the advertising business out of the boy…*

They passed a sign that said "Welcome to Illinois, the Land of Lincoln".

"We're almost there," said Azriel, remembering the terrain. They were near the giant Belasco woods that covered southwestern Indiana and southeastern Illinois.

Those woods had countless bodies and dark secrets buried there. Azriel used to hear adults nervously say that if you listened closely, you could hear men and women and children screaming amongst the rustling branches on a windy day.

Those woods were menacing.

But to Azriel, they felt like home.

- 2 -

The next day they made it to Belasco's eastern entrance on Anders Street, which would lead them to Hove Street, from which they could go downtown.

Azriel could have given Finius a heads up he was coming. But something told him not to. Azriel never trusted Finius, and still didn't. Roper didn't either. Even after their team-up against Rood and Fezziwig, where Finius helped him save the world, Azriel didn't trust the man. Finius wasn't exactly evil, as far as Azriel was concerned. But he was ruthless and misguided and sociopathic. *Chaotic neutral, would be his* Dungeons & Dragons *alignment*, Azriel guessed. Either way, they were three attributes that, when used together, caused bad things to happen. Just like when Finius awakened the zombie menace just to force Azriel into the game of being the Predator he was born to be.

"Are you okay, Love?" asked Dotty.

She noticed Azriel deep in thought with a grimace on his face. Azriel's anger both frightened and aroused her. Every day men hit on her when out feeding the homeless or running errands. Yet, no man had ever been truly attractive to her until Azriel. There was something about him she couldn't help but love. She just wanted to hug and take care of him. Thoughts of being with him even distracted her prayer time, something that had never happened before.

"I'm fine. But listen, we need to be careful. Finius is... *slippery*. Can't be trusted."

"I know," she replied. "He used to give me candy and gifts when I was a little girl. Although I used to sneeze around him a lot, like when around dogs since I'm allergic. It was weird. Daddy and him used to fight a lot until he banished Finius from the Order. Daddy says he's a twisted son of a bee sting."

"I trust him about as far as I can take a piss," said Azriel clenching his fists, and ignoring his inner profanity editor around Dotty. His violent temper bubbled under the surface. He always got a strange feeling from Finius. Since Finius was part zombie, that only made sense. But it was more than that. Finius always had the air about him as if he knew something you didn't, and was plotting to use that something *against* you. It was a lesson Pastor Shane learned the hard way when Finius pushed him into the zombies so he could save his own life.

"That's weird, look at that..." said Azriel.

"What is it?" asked Dotty.

There was a giant sailboat parked on the on ramp from highway 57.

"Rood's sailboat. Finius never moved it. Wonder who that is standing next to it?"

There was a tall figure standing up against the boat. As they walked up to him, they noticed he didn't move. He wore a straw hat, his mouth was wide open, and he wore a cheap suit — like a car salesman or a broke newbie politician.

"Hey," said Azriel touching the man's arm.

The man fell to the ground and the straw hat fell off him.

Dotty let out a nervous giggle.

"What's so funny?" asked Azriel.

"He reminds me of a scene in a movie Daddy loves. Where a couple garbage men disguise the dead mayor they found in a garbage can with a hat just like that."

Azriel glared at her with a look that said, *Are you serious?* "He's dead." Azriel kneeled down looking closer at the body. The man's skin was pale.

Almost white. He had two fang bite marks in his neck.

"Vampires. *Balls!*"

- 3 -

"Listen Dotty, I think this town may be in trouble still. I'm not sure what's going on. It's daylight so we're safe for now. But stay close."

"Okay."

Azriel decided to go to Pastor Shane's church first.

If there was a safe place in town, that church should be it. Roper said it was holy ground. Not that that stopped the zombie cop and vampires from desecrating the place. But if the demons were hot on their trail — and they still didn't know, either way — that'd be the safest place.

Belasco's streets looked dead as ever.

A true ghost town.

Or monster town, thought Azriel.

The church looked just as it had before:

Rawger's squad car was still parked outside with the deflated tires. The front door was still missing. And the pews and objects inside were still in shambles from his fights with Rawger and, later, the vampires.

It was as if Finius wasn't even there anymore and just left the town altogether.

Or maybe he was running *from* something…

Azriel led Dotty to the stairway that went down to the basement and Pastor Shane's panic room. The stairway was still demolished from the fight with Chief Rawger. And as soon as Azriel knelt down to poke his head into the dark — his eyes glowed red and his night vision kicked in. That usually only happened when he was under stress. Stress, this time, caused by that internal alarm in his body telling him monsters were around.

"Dotty, I want you to go outside. Wait for me. If you see or hear anything scream as loud as you can and I'll come for you."

"No Love, we need to stick together. Don't separate us."

"I have to see what's going on. There are monsters in there. Maybe lots of them. I'll be okay. I'm not going to attack them, I just want to take a *peek*. Wait outside. Go."

Dotty walked down the aisle of pews and stood by the doorway. She noticed how familiar everything looked. She had dreams about Azriel fighting a zombie in this church when she was a child years before the event took place. The memories returned to her like someone remembering a movie they once saw as a kid.

Azriel hopped down into the basement on top of the broken staircase. He could feel whatever was down there right up ahead. The monsters were behind where Pastor Shane's panic room door used to be. The door was destroyed when Rood's bitch concubine Mara and Azriel's own treacherous so-called grandma ambushed him.

The anger and rage Azriel felt whenever he even so much as saw a picture of a monster, much less was approaching one, burned like acid in his veins. Not being one for sneaking around he decided screw it — he'd barge in.

Sorry Dotty, I lied. I'm not just going to take a peek, I'm going to do some poking, *too.*

He ran into the panic room, giving fully into his instincts, to attack, mutilate, and kill whatever was inside.

- 4 -

I didn't see that *coming,* thought Azriel.

Pastor Shane's panic room looked completely different. The bookcases, and table, and chairs were all gone. Instead, there was a metal table with thick chains bolted into the ground and ceiling. It looked like something right out of a mad scientist's lab. There was a long figure on the table that looked like a bald man with gray skin at first glance. But as Azriel walked up to it, he noticed it wasn't flesh skin. It was pure rock. The thing was at least 8-feet tall, had stone for skin, and was missing its right arm. Its remaining left arm had six fingers, and both feet had six toes.

It lay completely still.

No, can't be dead. If he was dead I wouldn't sense his presence, thought Azriel touching the skin. It was definitely rock. It was jagged, too. *This would hurt like a son-of-a-bitch if it hit someone.*

The monster's large left arm was hooked up to both chains.

Azriel noticed a single book on the ground near the table. He picked it up and looked at the title. It was *Frankenstein* by Mary Shelly. A page was marked with a paperclip. Azriel opened it and there was a passage marked in yellow highlighter that said:

"The fallen angel becomes a malignant devil. Yet even that enemy of God and man had friends and associates in his desolation; I am alone."

Azriel put the book back down.

"Strange," he said aloud. "What kind of sick demented shit are you up to, Finius?"

Azriel heard movement on the table.

A low, growling noise sounded. The shackled arm shot up, yanking at the chains, ripping them out of the rings they were bolted to on the ground and the ceiling.

"You!" said the rock-skinned giant getting up off the table. "You took it! You took my arm! Give it back!"

The monster ripped the shackle clamp off his wrist and dropped it on the floor with a pile of chain. Then Azriel noticed movement on the monster's shoulder on the armless side. It looked like a wave of its rock-flesh moving up from his chest to his shoulder. A little girl's head and torso — made of the same rock-like substance as the monster's flesh — popped up. It was just a torso, arms, and head. Its torso was attached to the monster's shoulder.

"Pappy get him!" it said. "Get him! Get him! Get him! Then we'll *eat* him!" The child-thing laughed an awful, high pitched sound that made Azriel want to rip the little bitch right out of the rock-skinned monster's body.

- 5 -

Azriel wasted no time attacking.

Unlike the demon-possessed children, there was no reason to hold back on this thing. No reason to restrain himself. He let loose punching and kicking and attacking. The rock monster was on the ground before it had a chance to swing its one good arm. Azriel wailed on the rocky face and its grotesque child. Rock chips and bits flew off in both directions with each blow.

Then the appendage-child stopped yelling and bit Azriel on the ear.

"Ow!" said Azriel looking at the thing. His ear was bleeding.

"Get off my Pappy! Get off my Pappy!!" she screamed.

Azriel shifted his arm to punch the appendage-child. But before he could, the rock man's good arm connected with his jaw.

The monster hit Azriel so hard he soared into the metal table knocking it over.

The rock monster leaped to its feet. Its one arm was huge. At least twice as big as the arms Azriel saw on dudes who competed in Olympic weightlifting on TV. The appendage-child attached to it was screaming and yelling saying she was hungry and, "Let's eat him, Pappy, let's *EAT* HIM!"

Azriel hopped to his feet and attacked again.

This time, he dove into the rock monster with his shoulder and pushed him as hard as he could into the wall, crashing into the cement, with the child rock girl's head smashing into it.

The small rock head fell off and onto the floor into dozens of pieces.

The fragments reformed into the girl's head on their own. The eyes opened and continued screaming. "Pappy get him! Get him Pappy! I'm hungry! GET HIM!"

What the hell is this thing, thought Azriel, as he dodged a punch from the still-standing rock monster, then countered by kicking it in the leg, knocking it onto its rear.

The rock monster jumped up and ran towards the doorway. Azriel picked the still-screaming child-head up and chased after him.

Then a thought:

Balls! Dotty's up there!

\- 6 -

"Dotty watch out!" yelled Azriel as loud as he could as he jumped up into the church through the broken stairway opening. The rock monster was at the door. Dotty screamed as it grabbed her arm. Azriel knew it wouldn't take much for it to crush Dotty's arm — or entire body — if it wished.

Azriel wound up like a baseball pitcher about to throw a fastball, and chucked the still-yelling head — *Get her Pappy! Get her! Let's EAT* her, *too!* — at the rock monster as hard as he could. It connected with the rock man's back and shattered into small particles of dust and debris. It didn't reform itself.

"That ought to shut her stupid yap," said Azriel.

The rock monster looked at the head and howled and tried to backhand Dotty. Dotty ducked on pure instinct. The rock monster's arm hit the church doorway, smashing a big hole in the frame.

Azriel dove at its legs, bringing it to the ground.

It connected another punch to Azriel, this time on top of his head.

Azriel thought it felt like his skull had just been dented.

The rock monster looked at the head and howled and tried to backhand Dotty. Dotty ducked on pure instinct. The rock monster's arm hit the church doorway, smashing a big hole in the already-damaged door frame.

Azriel dove at the rock-monster's legs, bringing it to the ground.

It connected another punch to Azriel, this time on top of his head.

Azriel thought it felt like his skull had just been dented.

The rock monster kicked Azriel off him and ran down the street. Azriel sat up, rubbing his head.

"Get him, Love. Get him!" said Dotty.

Azriel smiled.

He was *really* starting to like this girl!

Azriel ran after the rock monster. It headed towards the police station. *Why there, of all places*, thought Azriel as he gained on it. He was running almost faster than a racecar with his superhuman speed. Azriel was almost upon the rock monster when it ran into the big doorway that was smashed by Finius's truck years earlier.

Azriel followed it inside.

He saw it going for the stairway down to the jail cells.

Of course… has to be the jails, thought Azriel.

Azriel's most gruesome and disturbing memories were of that fucking jail. Rawger had him chained there, eating people right in front of him. Azriel could still remember like it was yesterday. Rawger was almost 20-feet tall by then. He ate men, women, and children. Rawger's body grew stronger and taller with every swallow of flesh. Azriel felt like puking at the thought of when Rawger would talk to him with his mouth full of bits and pieces of bone and brain and entrails spraying out as he spoke. Then, later, Rood tried to skin Azriel alive in that same building to carve a *sailboat* into his flesh and drain his blood out to soup himself up with power.

And now, here he was again.

Great.

Azriel paused for a second to reflect upon all this. But his anger quickly outweighed his aversion to the jail. He darted down the stairs after the rock monster.

- 7 -

Azriel ran into the jail room and cornered the rock monster.

It was using its arm to pull the jail cell doors off the hinges as if they were made of paper. One by one he tore the cell doors off and tossed them at Azriel who just barely managed to dodge them. Inside the first cell was a large dog with glowing orange eyes. It was skinny, and looked pure evil. But it was chained inside the cell and couldn't get out. It snapped and growled.

Azriel ignored it and sped across the room towards the rock monster and dived at his legs again, taking him to the floor. Azriel pounded on its face as hard has he could. He ignored how each punch ripped the skin off his knuckles. He just kept hitting and hitting and hitting the rock monster's face until its face fell off and into several pieces, like the appendage-baby that grew out of his shoulder. The rock monster's body convulsed, then went still. To make sure the job was finished Azriel grabbed its one arm, ripped it off and smashed it into the wall into several pieces. Then, he did the same to its legs and stomped on the pieces until they were but gravel.

Azriel's rage remained. He couldn't satisfy his anger. He just wanted to kill and kill and keep killing monsters.

He looked around the jail cells

Each cell was packed with various monsters who were either dead or not moving. Some of the monsters inside he'd heard of just from movies and popular culture. Some he'd never seen before. All were apparently dead and deformed, with body parts missing, blood drained into stained buckets, guts spilling out, and various appendages lying around.

The putrid smell was near intolerable.

Azriel saw a body with a bull's head on it, on the ground, dead in one cell. He saw things that looked like ghouls, things that were scaly, things that were half man, half animal. There was a naked woman with horns on her head and big breasts lying in the corner, with two broken-looking appendages in her back that looked like they had been wings that were yanked out.

It looked like only two things in the entire jail were still alive or moving. One was the starving horse-sized dog with the glowing eyes snapping and snarling, but still chained in its cell. The other was a green monster, tall and lanky — it looked like it was starving. Azriel could see its spine poking through its skinny back. It looked like there was just one layer of skin separating his bones from the outside. It had a long square nose. It was in one of the few cells the rock monster didn't rip the door off of. The monster was holding the bars and talking.

It said in a perfect English accent: "Fancy a fuck, mate?"

"What?"

"How about you let me fuck you then eat you. Or perhaps just an appendage? A leg would do," it licked its pursed lips. "Not even your *whole* leg. I just need a morsel, mate. Do me a solid and I'll give you something big and solid. Throw a troll a bone. I'm boney and have a big boner, see?" It pulled its pants down and showed a large stiff green penis. It tapped its erect dick on the cell like a prison guard rattling a nightstick on jail bars.

"I'd make you eat *that* first, Bunky," said Azriel.

"Watch out!" the monster said.

"What?"

"I smell something, mate. I think *he's* coming back! I think the zombie man is coming back!" The troll ran to his cell's corner, walking over the lifeless bodies and carcasses of other monsters and organs and innards. His boner went down into the shape of a flaccid green broken rubber band.

Azriel clenched his fists and prepared for battle.

If this was Finius, hopefully the slippery man didn't intend to fight or Azriel would be in trouble. Every time Azriel tried fighting Finius he got his ass handed to him. *I really need to learn how to fight*, he thought again as the door opened.

"That you Finius, you freaky fuck!" said Azriel.

"Language, Azriel. Enough with the language," said an old man's voice Azriel instantly recognized.

It was Roper.

The old man limped in, wearing his usual all-denim attire. "I would have made it sooner but Bullinger's engine ended up croaking on me. Had to limp and thumb my way here. Took a dog's age."

Dotty ran in from behind her father towards Azriel. She embraced him and kissed him on his mouth.

11
GRANNY'S PLAYTHING

"The brain is a machine that a ghost can operate."

- Sir John Eccles
Nobel Prize-Winning Neurophysiologist

- 1 -

When Rapha told the wraith who he wanted to possess to help him kill the Predator, the wraith — who always somehow knew where the soon-to-be hosts were — gave him her coordinates:

A hospital in a small Oregon town called DaBeach.

Rapha could move anywhere he wanted on the planet at the speed of thought — whether one foot away or ten thousand miles away. And while he perpetually thirsted for inhabiting a flesh body, and was distracted by that thirst and hated needing it so much, he found this particular demonic attribute helpful.

The wraith knew exactly what hospital, on what wing, and in what room his host was. Being one of Abaddon's earthly servants, it had many connections throughout the spirit world, as well as in the world of Nephilim. He prided himself on being able to access information faster than the Internet *"and without the bandwidth problems."*

Rapha found many cracks through which to enter the hospital.

No invitation was necessary.

The hospital was full of people so desperate to save their sick and dying loved ones, they resorted to all kind of pagan idolatry and appeals to false gods. Some of them were even praying to demons under the guise of various Eastern religions.

Rapha floated down the halls towards his soon-to-be host. He knew three things about her. One, she was one of the most feared Predators of all. She was probably even stronger than Lucifer's favorite. At least, until Azrael learned how to unleash the powers trapped inside him. Secondly, she hated Azrael as much as Rapha and Arba did — but for different reasons. After accessing Azrael's mind Rapha saw them fight in a bar near the hospital. Rapha tasted the raw contempt and hatred this woman had for Azrael. It was spicy. Third, and best of all, she had the same goal he did:

To destroy Lucifer's favorite by any means necessary.

Her superhuman Predator body and hatred for their shared enemy would make her an excellent host indeed. She could possibly even give

Rapha the power to destroy Arba, too, and ensure he won Abaddon's favor.

Rapha hovered over her comatose body. The bed was too short for her huge frame. Her feet and ankles below the knees dangled over the edge. She was wearing a hospital gown and her body was hooked up to various tubes, scopes, and monitors. She was breathing via the machines hooked up to her. But her subconscious was very much alive. She was dreaming about a cartoon from her youth called "Casper the Friendly Ghost" and oblivious to Rapha's presence. Rapha would access her mind to find the information he needed to persuade her to his cause. Or, if all else failed, manipulate her into his cause. Same outcome either way.

Rapha prepared to read the Predator woman's mind, while hidden from her consciousness. He would reveal himself to her at the right time when he had what he needed.

First, he had work to do.

He couldn't afford any mistakes and needed to gather info.

He began reading her thoughts, memories, fears, hopes, and desires going all the way back to when she was in her mother's womb.

- 2 -

The Predator's name was Olga.

She was from an Eastern European country so obscure, it's not on any maps. Her mother died at childbirth after Olga used her enormous feet and unusual strength to kick a hole right through her stomach during the birth, while chewing the umbilical cord off. Olga was born with her adult teeth already in place and chewed on the cord like it was a long piece of licorice.

The midwife who delivered Olga fainted at the sight of it. The large child wriggled out of her mother's belly, dropped off the delivery table, and crawled outside the house, pushing the door down off its hinges.

She scrabbled to the nearby woods where, naked and still drenched in embryonic fluid, she attracted a starving coyote's attention. The coyote attacked the baby. It bit and snapped at her neck, causing scars that her still-emerging Predator abilities were never able to fully heal.

The coyote sensed people coming. It bit onto Olga's chubby long leg and tried to drag her deeper into the forest where it could enjoy its meal without interruption. The approaching people were no doubt looking for the child.

As the coyote dragged baby Olga into the forest, she flailed her arms and free leg. She then instinctively grabbed for the coyote's back paw and, with her superhumanly strong grip, crushed it.

The coyote howled and tried limping away.

Olga crawled after it, faster than the coyote could limp. She grabbed its tail and yanked it back towards her. Then, with her chubby baby hands,

Olga plucked both its eyes out with a giggle.

The coyote howled again.

The child pried the coyote's mouth open — one of her hands on the top part of its snout, the other hand on the bottom — and pushed, breaking its jaw.

She giggled again.

The coyote slumped over and blacked out from pain and shock.

The less-than-an-hour old baby Olga realized she was still hungry. She looked at the wounded coyote. Her senses heard its heart slow down and the life leave it.

She giggled again, then prepared to eat her second meal.

- 3 -

Baby Olga was eating the coyote's heart when the midwife and search party found her. She was smiling and cooing as she ate sitting in a pile of her own excrement.

Nobody knew what the child was.

Some of the people said she was a demon.

Some said she was "special."

And one person wanted to kill her saying she was the devil's child.

The midwife said she did not know who the father was. But the mother had been raped nine months earlier. The mother didn't even know the man's name or whereabouts. Only that he was unusually strong and cruel.

Whoever the father was, the child was an orphan now and who would claim her?

The midwife decided to take the child in and love her and protect her. And, if possible, help her.

That same night a hunched over old woman entered the town. She was covered head to toe in baggy clothes, and hid most of her face and head with a black shawl. She went immediately to the midwife and demanded custody of the child, who was in the crib, already almost too big for it.

When the midwife asked the old woman her name and who she was, the old woman pulled off her shawl. She looked ancient — like a living mummy. She had dry leathery skin, pursed lips, barely any nose to speak of, and was covered in deep wrinkles.

The old woman replied:

"Call me *Granny.*" She then picked up the large infant, flashed a mostly-toothless smile, and cackled.

- 4 -

When the midwife saw the decrepit old woman's dark eyes and sinister smile, she immediately screamed out the window for help. The town constable was nearby and rushed over.

An argument ensued.

Other men and women came over to see the commotion. There was a crowd around the woman's door and windows within minutes. This kind of excitement had not happened in that town in decades. They didn't even have TV in the village.

After much arguing and threats — many of the threats sexual in nature, Rapha noted — by the old woman, the matter was settled: The child would stay unless the old woman could show proof of her being the child's grandmother.

The old woman threatened to rape the constable and make a necklace out of the midwife's teeth. Then she put her shawl back on and left. She cackled loudly, as if she knew something the townsfolk didn't.

The infant Olga couldn't sleep that night.

She sensed a coming disturbance.

Something violent was about to happen. It made her feel excited.

At midnight the old woman kicked the door in. She was holding a pair of pliers. She walked past baby Olga, gave her a glance and a cackle, and told her to "sit tight little fledgling, your ever-lovin' Granny will be back for you in a jiffy!"

The old woman entered the midwife's room.

There was screaming.

The old woman's voice said, "Only 25 more teeth to go!" Then a scream. Then, "Only 24 more teeth to go!" then another scream, and so on, counting down every time she plucked one of the midwife's teeth out. The screaming led to people coming inside the broken-down door. Baby Olga watched, without making a sound, enjoying the spectacle, as the old woman who called herself Granny started fighting the entire horde of townsfolk.

Baby Olga watched Granny punch holes through peoples' chests.

She twisted their heads off their bodies and pulled their heads out still attached to their spines.

She jumped around, dodging blows and gunfire, and by the time she was done everyone in the town was dead. To make sure everyone was dead, she went house to house, and slaughtered anyone she found hiding — men, women, and children — while cackling the whole time.

Then Granny returned to the midwife's house and picked baby Olga up. Granny's hands and arms were covered in blood. She looked like she was wearing crimson wet sleeves.

"There, there, see how that's done my little *plaything*? You'll be able to do these things too! But not to people like this. Do them to much scarier things. Granny is here, little fledgling. Granny is here to take care of you!"

The old woman kept cackling as she carried baby Olga outside, walking over all the bodies of the people she killed that night.

- 5 -

Rapha found those first unconscious memories amusing. But they didn't give him the information he needed to bargain for control over Olga's spirit and body and operate her brain.

He skipped ahead to her future memories.

Her first conscious memory was when she was three years old. She was being beaten and slapped by Granny — *The 'Nana*, as the old woman had Olga call her — and starved. Granny called Olga her "plaything" and rarely ever fed her. And what Granny did manage to feed Olga was always a live rodent the child was expected to kill and eat raw.

Granny also started teaching Olga how to fight.

She taught her fighting styles and moves from all over the world.

Olga often wondered how old Granny was. When she once asked, Granny said she was *older than she felt and younger than she smelt* and left it at that.

Olga could never seem to please Granny who constantly berated her, belittled her, and rejected her — even going so far as to tell child Olga she wasn't her real grandma. And even if she had been her real grandma she'd be ashamed at what a pussy Olga was.

Olga didn't like eating rodents. But eventually she learned to find and catch her own food in the big city they lived in. She enjoyed using her strength and power to survive. Granny would sometimes drop her off in obscure parts of town where monsters roamed and tell her she either fought her way out or would die. Olga loved every minute of it. She enjoyed fighting monsters while Granny watched. There was something *pure* about it. And she desperately wanted Granny's approval. But she never got it. Instead, after every fight, Granny would tell her to do better next time or she'd kill her little plaything herself.

Rapha found these memories boring.

He needed a hook.

He needed some kind of hold he could use to exploit Olga to get her to agree to allow him to possess her body, willingly, without fighting him or trying to cast him out. Rapha would need his full concentration when fighting Lucifer's favorite, and her constantly battling him for control would not work. Especially if he was to destroy Arba, too, who he had no illusions wasn't plotting to do the same to him.

Rapha went into Olga's more recent memories.

And while looking at them, he finally saw the hook — big and gleaming — he was looking for.

- 6 -

When Olga became a teenager, growing both in stature and maturity, Granny started visiting her bedroom at night and molesting her.

It was shameful and humiliating.

But Olga was so desperate for Granny's approval she went along with it hoping Granny would finally give her a compliment.

During these years she felt her body changing. The longer Granny's nighttime visits went on… the more the men Olga's teenage mind had once found attractive no longer were. She laid up at night, dreading Granny's entrance, and always thinking, *my body is betraying me…* whenever she tried to force herself to find men attractive. But she couldn't. Something Granny did to her — was still doing to her — was wiping out her desire for men. That desire was replaced by an emptiness she wanted to fill by giving in to her violent nature and tendencies. As Olga got older, she knew it was deliberate. Granny was preparing her for something. And night by night, Granny went into her room and fondled Olga's now fully-matured breasts. She would lick and kiss Olga with her old, sagging mouth and breath that smelled so bad it made Olga want to throw up. Granny would tell Olga how badly she wanted to fuck her little *plaything* now that she was finally a woman. Olga found Granny disgusting. But if this was the only approval she could get from her, then so be it. She could live with that. And maybe, just maybe, Granny would leave her alone if she submitted to the visits instead of fighting her.

But Granny rarely left Olga alone.

Not for the three years between her 16th and 19th birthdays.

At that time, Olga couldn't stomach Granny anymore and started trying to fight back. But even as Olga's strength and power increased, Granny still always overcame her. Granny insisted Olga wear Cubs and Green Bay Packers apparel, saying it made her look sexy. Everything about the old woman was *sex*. The 'Nana was obsessed with it. She was particularly obsessed with raping people. And the more Olga struggled, the more Granny liked it. It was the only approval Olga got from Granny.

As the years went on and Olga grew to her full height of 7'9, her arms and legs filling out, becoming even stronger and tougher (*If you were a man, you'd be hung like a tree trunk,* Granny would tell her) Granny started losing interest in molesting Olga. Instead, Granny would bring men home — bound and gagged, with the occasional willing partner — and rape them right in front of her, cackling and laughing and enjoying it.

One night around ten years before Rapha's hospital visit, she brought a man home Olga instantly didn't like.

The man had a slick smile and wore a long black trench coat. He called himself "Finius." There was something about him Olga instantly hated — a feeling in her gut. It was similar but not exactly the same as the feeling monsters gave her when she fought them with Granny. It made her angry and want to lash out and kill something. Granny noted it and told her "he's not who we hunt."

Olga watched Granny and Finius have sex that night.

They played vampire with each other, drinking each other's blood and talking with fake Transylvanian accents.

Later that night when Granny was asleep, Finius went into Olga's bedroom. He sprayed some kind of blue powder on her from a can. Olga's entire body was filled with pain. She felt like she wanted to throw up. Her head felt like little daggers were jabbing inside her brain on all softest points. She couldn't even move, much less resist the man with the slick smile.

"I went all the way to Mount Hermon in the Holy Land to get this," said the creepy man Finius. "I know it hurts. But don't worry, it doesn't hurt me a bit." The man jabbed a long needle into Olga's arm. "You Predators have such tough skin, without this ghastly blue power I would need a power drill."

Olga's scream woke Granny up. She yelled at the man Finius, and told him to leave or she'd fuck him to death. They briefly fought. Furniture was thrown around. Granny was strong and tough. But this Finius guy was fast and nimble. *Slippery*, Granny said.

The man sprayed the same blue powder substance on Granny.

Granny became as helpless as Olga. She writhed in agony on the floor next to her plaything. The only difference was, Granny wasn't crying from the pain, she was cackling. A pained cackle, but a cackle all the same.

Finius left after beating Granny into submission.

Granny looked sad the next day and never touched Olga again after that. She then told Olga it was time for her little plaything to fly the coop. To hunt down and kill monsters on her own. To fulfill the purpose Granny had prepared her for. "Forget about sex and fucking men or women… take it from me little plaything, it's a waste of life. Go and prey on monsters. You need to toughen up. And maybe someday you'll make me proud. But I'm not holding my breath waiting. You've been nothing but a disappointment so far. As useless to the cause as one of the monsters we prey on."

Olga found that an odd thing for Granny to say considering she was the ultimate monster. Yet, even after all the pain Granny caused her, Olga still needed Granny's approval. And she vowed to get it. And once she got Granny's approval, she would kill the old deranged hag. Such was the way Predator families behaved towards one another.

- 7 -

Rapha skipped ahead to Olga's most recent memory and another hook he could use:

Her fight with Azriel.

Olga had spent the last few years making a name for herself amongst the other Predators. The monsters feared her. Granny had trained her up to be the most deadly of them all. Even other Predators feared her. But when she had gotten a lead on where Lucifer's favorite was — the Predator destined to turn on his own kind and hunt them down, instead of the monsters — she made it her all-consuming priority to find and kill him.

She searched for Lucifer's favorite for months. Through many dark channels, she discovered the Predator was still young — just a teenager. She eventually found out he was in a small town called Belasco. She tried to find Granny for help just in case she would need backup. But Granny was nowhere to be found. Granny had gone dark. So Olga went alone.

When she got to Belasco, nobody was there. The entire town was destroyed. The woods were burnt down in many areas. Rumors from other Predators were that Lucifer's favorite had destroyed the town along with all the zombies in it.

Olga continued to look for him.

She sought out the head of the Order — an old man named Roper. Granny had told her many times never to contact Roper and stay away from the Order. But Olga was desperate. She needed to be the one to kill Lucifer's favorite. However, Roper had no information to share. He said he heard the boy had gone soft and pacifist and was in *Canada*, but good luck finding him.

Olga harbored a lot of pain and resentment for Granny, who violated her and stole her innocence, but she still craved Granny's approval. She was obsessed with getting it. She couldn't kill Granny until she got the sick woman's approval, first. And what better way to get Granny's approval than to kill Lucifer's favorite? He was the biggest monster of them all.

Rapha found it amusing Olga did not know Granny was dead by then and would never get her approval even after she helped him kill Lucifer's favorite. But there was no reason to reveal that tidy bit of news to her, was there?

Then one day, Olga got a lead.

Someone named Azriel — a slightly different spelling of the name he was usually called by the Predators — was living on the Oregon coast.

She tracked him to a small town called DaBeach.

She immediately despised the town.

Too pleasant, she thought.

But it was so small she easily found Azriel and had almost beaten him.

But Azriel got the upper hand and beat Olga to what he thought was death. Rapha remembered this fight from when he possessed Azriel's mind. Azriel thought at the time Olga had died.

But she didn't die and was taken to this hospital in town.

And here she lay unconscious — beaten, blinded, and crippled, according to the doctors. Although they said she had a remarkable recovery and it was a miracle she was alive. They didn't see her condition getting better. Rapha could tell Azriel beat Olga so badly, even her Predator body couldn't heal itself completely in her spine, legs, eyes, heart, and one of her arms.

Rapha had all the information he needed.

He knew Olga's insecurities, her needs, and her main desires and goals.

He had found the hook and now he had the bait.

At last, he decided to introduce himself to her.

Rapha invaded Olga's thoughts of *Casper the Friendly Ghost* and told her who he was, and that he too wanted to kill Lucifer's favorite. If they worked together there was a 93.987% chance they would win. He would help her get Granny's approval. He knew where Granny was and could help Olga find her. Then they would kill Granny. It would be easy with their combined might.

Rapha said he could also make Olga whole and give her mobility and sight again. Even her healing powers couldn't un-cripple her from the spinal injuries or restore her eyesight. The doctors said she would not be able to move anything below her neck. She could either let Rapha operate her brain and body or lie there, like a starfish, for the next several centuries — as Predators live long, unnatural lives. She would die with the full knowledge that Lucifer's favorite would live and that she could have helped kill him. She would live with the knowledge that her inaction would help the evil one complete his destiny. She would never get Granny's approval if that happened.

"What is your riposte, madam?" said Rapha to Olga's spirit.

Olga answered: "I give you complete control of my body, which I can no longer use anymore, and you swear we will kill Lucifer's favorite together? After that you will leave me, heal me, and we become enemies again?"

"Yes. If that is what you desire."

"But we kill Lucifer's favorite? We cut off his head and display it for the other monsters to see?"

"But of course. It will be my absolute pleasure to do this with you, madam," said Rapha.

"Then I say yes."

12
LUNATICK

"I shall have to invent a new classification of a lunatic for you."

- Doctor Jack Seward
Bram Stoker's *Dracula*

- 1 -

Arba traveled to Chicago at the speed of thought.

But he was so anxious, even that speed wasn't fast enough for him. He was almost giddy about who his new host would be, and *what* it would be.

When reading Azriel's mind, he knew his new host would have a special hatred for Azriel. A hatred which would give him power to kill the Predator more easily than any human host. It was such a perfect match; it was almost like God was on Arba's side.

He knew that wasn't the case, of course.

But isn't it amusing how things work out?

The host was not only a Nephilim monster, but Arba had known the host's father in life thousands of years earlier. Arba had always respected the host's father. And if the host was even half as devious, ferocious, bloodthirsty, and violent as its father, it would give Arba a huge advantage when he added his demonically-enhanced power to the host's monstrous strength and abilities.

Arba didn't even need to know his host's exact coordinates. He could tell by the shape of the tall building — the tallest building in the city — and by the host's father's name being boldly carved into the building's side.

Arba knew the name well:

FENRIS.

It pleased Arba to know that somehow Fenris — the first werewolf — had survived all these centuries. And it also pleased Arba that this was Fenris's building, Fenris's city, and it was Fenris's son he would be possessing.

- 2 -

"No deal, you filth," growled Fenris.

Arba had just manifested himself to the werewolf and made his request. Fenris shot the request down without even a moment's consideration.

"Now go. I don't want your kind *polluting* my stronghold or my only remaining son. He's not much. Just a runt. And a disappointment in every way. But he's all I have left. You touch him, demon, and I'll make anything Abaddon did to you in the pit feel like a grooming."

Fenris stood over eight feet tall. His six-fingered hands had large sharp claws that he liked to click together when in thought. He wore an expensive dress shirt and perfectly polished shoes. His pants were held up by suspenders. His long hair was pulled back tight. If Arba had seen the movie *Wall Street*, he'd have thought Fenris was a werewolf version of Gordon Gekko.

Arba was shocked at the response.

He had counted on getting the father's approval without resistance.

And why wouldn't he get it?

He read Azriel's memories. Azriel wiped out an entire party of Fenris's kind. And if nothing else, Fenris had always been a wheeling-and-dealing kind of monster. He loved to make deals. It's probably how he become so wealthy as far as Arba was concerned. And surely the werewolf could use a favor from a demon. But, even more importantly, Azriel killed Fenris's older son and heir to the empire. Why wouldn't he sacrifice his younger son's autonomy — especially if it was temporary? Of course, Arba never intended it to be temporary. But there was no way Fenris would know that. So why not let him possess his son to help kill the very Predator who mocked, humiliated, and hurt him?

It didn't make any sense.

"You are done here," said Fenris staring out his office window. He was still looking at the city — *his* city — back turned to Arba, hands behind his back, clicking his long claws. He seemed immune to the usual terror and fear that happened — even in monsters — a demon's presence created.

Arba bowed and floated out of the room.

He was not going to get the father's permission. And it was a pity. It would have made it so much easier to convince the son to let Arba possess him, and attach himself to the son's spirit.

Arba knew he would still get to his destination.

He'd just have to go the *scenic* route.

It was time for Plan B, he realized, as he darted out of the room to the boy werewolf's chambers.

- 3 -

Arba was as disappointed with the boy werewolf as the father was.

When Arba found his quarters in the giant Fenris tower he realized the boy was even shorter than what Azriel's memories suggested. He seemed to lack anything remotely resembling one of the great werewolf warriors of old. In life, Arba and his Anakim giant tribe gave a wide berth to the werewolves. Of all the were-creatures spawned by whichever fallen angel sired them during their second erruption after the Flood, the werewolves were the strongest, most fierce, and deadly. Even just a small band of them could wipe out entire giant and monster clans with relative ease. And they were especially powerful during full moons — when their strength, ferociousness, and speed doubled.

The werewolves were always terrifying and a little crazy.

But during full moons?

They were what the ancients called:

"Lunatik."

But this boy?

He *was* a runt. Just like his father said. And instead of his quarters being decorated with the skulls and bones of his victims and his furniture being draped with captive women, his room was decorated with... comic books. Cartoon and movie character posters adorned his walls. Toys and action figures were strewn around the floor. And when Arba entered the chambers he saw the boy hard at work drawing what looked to be a comic book. His long clawed hands were having trouble holding the pencil as he sketched. He was drawing a comic book called "Garbage Man" — a superhero he created. The boy was drawing a panel where the Garbage Man hero was confronting a villain. The word balloon from the villain said, "Who are you?" and the word balloon above the hero said, "I'm Garbage Man... and I'm here to take out the trash!"

Gay, thought Arba.

The boy was runty, weak, and stupid.

Next thing you know the boy will be attending church, too, Arba mused.

Plus, there was nothing ferocious about him at all.

Nothing menacing.

He was smiling as he drew his comic book. His tongue stuck out a little on top of his lip as he drew and erased.

The boy was a geek. Not a warrior.

He was pacifist. Not a warmonger.

A disappointment. Not someone who would give Arba the satisfaction of killing the most powerful Predator who had ever lived.

This is going to be harder than I planned, thought Arba as he invaded the boy werewolf's mind. He needed to read his thoughts and memories and, hopefully, find a way to get this weak-minded, pathetic excuse for a werewolf to help him destroy Lucifer's favorite.

- 4 -

The boy werewolf's name was Skoll.

His earliest subconscious memory was right after being born. His mother — a human woman who had been concubined-up by Fenris — was taking him from his crib and escaping the large mansion she lived in. Baby Skoll's head was on her shoulder looking behind her. His werewolf senses were already so sharp he could hear her rapid heartbeat, smell the fear coming out of her pores, and taste the salt in the evaporating tears on her cheek.

His mother immediately met up with someone.

It was a man dressed in black with a big grin.

His mother called the man "Finius."

This man in black smelled different from his mother. He didn't smell like he was alive. But he didn't smell dead, either. If Skoll's infant mind could have processed it, he would have thought the man smelled not so much dead, but *not alive.* Skoll's mind didn't process any of this at the time, of course. But it was all there, in his subconscious, waiting to be accessed.

The man in black promised to help the woman.

To give her sanctuary.

To protect her from the were-creatures that no doubt had her scent and would easily find her anywhere in the world. The man in black told her you don't just take the king of the werewolves' child and think you're going to escape without assistance. He then said he could help her for a *price.*

"What price?" asked the woman.

"I want the boy's blood," said Finius.

"His blood?"

"Yes, and lots of it. Don't worry, I won't harm him. I will wait until he's older. At least a few *days* old. But I will need a lot of it. Is it a deal?"

The woman knew she had no choice.

She agreed to let the man take her son's blood in exchange for his help.

The man Finius took the woman and Skoll away on a boat and they floated around for a few days. The boat was dirty and it stank. The only thing to eat on the boat were vegetables and fruits which were rotting fast.

"I'm a vegetarian," said the man Finius when the woman complained that her son needed meat. Whenever the boy ate the produce, he threw it up, and it refused to stay down in his carnivorous werewolf digestive system. The boy would starve if he didn't get meat.

"Give the boy *suck*, then," said Finius.

"My milk doesn't sustain him either, he needs meat."

"Well then, you're the boy's mother, give him meat," said Finius as he spun a long sharp knife on the tip of his finger like a top, and handed it to the woman. "He's still small. A couple fingers ought to do."

That night Skoll had his first meal:

His mother's two index fingers.

- 5 -

After the infant's first week of life the man Finius said Skoll was finally old enough. He took the werewolf child's blood many times over the course of several days. Finius kept taking the blood until he had enough to fill a large jug of the orange colored liquid. After the last blood-drawing, he docked the boat and told the woman to get off and good luck. She yelled at him for not fulfilling his part of the bargain to protect them. But he simply laughed and told her good luck again, and sailed off — eyeing the jug of orange blood like a gold hunter finding a treasure.

It wasn't long after that — on the next full moon — when the boy's father's agents found them. When they were on the boat, the rotting vegetable and fruit smell covered their scents. When they landed, they were quickly found. The mother was decapitated on the spot. Skoll instinctively cried as he gnawed on one of her toe bones she had cut off for him to sup on.

The werewolves took baby Skoll away that night. The child screamed and lashed out with his small but sharp emerging claws. The lunatik full moon gave his infant-sized body unusual amounts of strength and power — even for a werewolf. Nobody there had ever seen a baby werewolf show so much rage and strength. He clawed at the were-creature's eye who took him from his mother, tearing it out.

The other werewolves nervously laughed and none of them wanted to hold him after that.

Arba found this memory amusing.

But it wasn't that helpful.

He needed an angle to go after this Skoll pup with.

Watching his mother die and how he reacted meant the child had the spark of that rage Arba wanted. But he needed something to trigger that internal werewolf blood lust that he should have but clearly didn't.

Arba continued reading Skoll's thoughts probing for that hook.

Arba found exactly what memories he was looking for during the werewolf's fifteenth year. Perhaps the boy wasn't as weak and useless as his father (or Arba) thought he was.

- 6 -

By his teen years, Skoll's interests had focused exclusively on all the sissy talents that his dad was embarrassed of his son for having.

They were all passive activities like reading and drawing and art and music. His father had started to suspect his son might be gay and, thus, had to be discarded, with no biological use whatsoever to the clan. Fenris decided to see if his instincts were correct and sent his youngest son on a date with a potential mate.

Skoll had shown little interest in women his entire life.

He liked girls a lot and fantasized about them all the time. But he was simply too shy and lacked confidence to do anything about his urges — even though he was the son of the first and most powerful werewolf.

To make sure Skoll didn't screw anything up, Fenris sent Skoll's older brother Warg to go with him.

Warg was the exact opposite of Skoll in every way. Warg was already turning into a mighty warrior by the time he was eight years old. He had mastered the arts and sciences of killing, stealth, and controlling his anger and emotions during the full moons. That was an especially dangerous time for both werewolves and those around them. During full moons werewolves went what they called "lunatik." Their blood lust at its highest, not thinking, just feeling, the very instincts that had gotten their kind discovered, hunted, and killed for thousands of years. Fenris had lost all his other sons over the centuries to this blood lust. And it wasn't until Fenris organized his kind into a pack and taught them how to survive and resist their full moon urges, that the werewolf legends ceased to exist, and their killings and rampages went underground.

But, for some reason, Skoll didn't have that lunatik urge.

Although some wondered if it was just being repressed. He certainly showed it as a baby.

Skoll knew his father didn't like him or respect him. But his brother Warg, did. Warg took care of Skoll, covered for him, and stood up for him to their father. Thus, Warg happily agreed to follow Skoll on his date that night.

To remain downwind, so Skoll couldn't catch his scent, and report back what he saw. The human girl Fenris – ever the deal maker – set his son up with was as excited as ever. She was pretty, rich, and her family wealth would make an excellent addition to Fenris's. Fenris thought the girl would make a fitting start for his son's harem should he prove not to be the sissy he acted like. The girl knew about Skoll's heritage and even found him and his werewolf attributes hot. She was anxious to be bitten and turned into a werewolf if she proved worthy. She had been raised to want a werewolf mate and child. Such were the business deals Fenris had set up for his kind to hide and thrive in a human-dominated world.

The date started off exactly as Fenris wanted it to.

Skoll and the girl, whose name was Chloe, went to dinner in a restaurant Fenris owned and were alone. Chloe didn't mind Skoll's appetite for bloody raw meat and it turned out they both had a love for comic books and Japanese animation.

They danced afterwards.

Chloe found the boy werewolf's clumsiness and lack of rhythm adorable.

They then took a long walk in the full moon light.

Fenris had never seen his son act Lunatik before and feared nothing. In fact, "Maybe it would give the little runt some backbone to fuck and impregnate his new concubine," he told his servants.

Skoll had never had such a great time.

He drank in the girl's sensuality through his senses.

He found it hard to stifle a boner. Chloe didn't notice as Skoll's penis was small compared to other werewolves. There was something about Chloe that was familiar to Skoll. He couldn't understand it. But Fenris had arranged hundreds of marriages in his pack over the centuries. And picking women that reminded werewolves of their human mothers almost always enhanced a werewolf's attraction and pheromone levels. And so it was with this human girl.

But when Chloe went in for a kiss, as Skoll was still too shy and scared to make a move, something happened.

Maybe it was his lack of experience kissing girls.

Maybe it was horniness.

Or maybe… it was the full moon.

But the boy werewolf bit Chloe's mouth with his fangs and drew blood. Chloe looked briefly turned on for a moment. A bite like that would surely turn her into a werewolf. It excited her!

But Skoll only felt hunger.

And rage.

There was something about the girl. He didn't know what. But Arba saw it clearly: She looked just like Skoll's mother. Skoll had tasted his mother's flesh. He watched her be killed in front of him. He had some kind of twisted internal lust for this girl suddenly. And as she licked her lips and puckered up for another kiss, Skoll bit off Chloe's nose and swallowed it.

Chloe screamed.

Blood shot out everywhere.

"Fuck me!" growled Skoll. His normally meek voice sounded violent and angry. "Fuck me! Fuck me *now*!" He ripped off Chloe's blouse and bra and felt her perfect breasts with his clawed hands. His claws sunk into her breasts. She was crying and pleading for him to stop. But he couldn't. All he wanted to do… all he could think to do… was to bite and fuck her. It was a lust that couldn't be controlled as the full moon light washed over him.

Warg sprang out of the shadows and pulled him off her.

"What are you doing?"

"I can't… help it! She's mine! Mine to fuck and protect!"

"You're not making any sense, get off her!"

Hidden thoughts, emotions, and memories flooded Skoll's mind. The taste of his mother's flesh fingers and toes. How his father rejected, mocked, and humiliated him at every opportunity. How other werewolves laughed at him, called him a pussy and, even worse, a *poodle* — the ultimate insult to a werewolf.

Skoll felt hate, and anger, and betrayal.

But not for his brother who was restraining him.

He loved his brother.

The girl Chloe died in front of them.

"Father might kill you for this!" said Warg. "Do you know who this girl is?"

"What do I do?" asked Skoll.

He was still feeling the anger and violence, but it was quickly being replaced by fear. He saw what his father had done to his enemies. He had overheard his father say the only thing his youngest son was good for was mating with this human girl who for some reason finds his runtiness attractive.

"I'll take care of it," said Warg. "We'll make up some story. Blame it on the ghouls. This looks like something they would do. Go, get out of here!"

Skoll ran home.

His brother's lie was seared into his head. His brother loved him, at least. And always had his back.

The next day, Fenris declared war with the ghouls. Graveyards were raided. Ghouls were rounded up and executed. And Fenris lectured his son on how disappointing he was not being able to fight to stop a weak little ghoul from killing his concubine.

"You're weak and pathetic and I am ashamed of you," said Fenris looking out his window and clicking his claws in his ever-calm state.

Once again, Warg stepped in.

He said some lie about how the ghoul wasn't alone and his brother fought bravely.

But Fenris didn't accept the lie.

That day he disowned his youngest son.

"You like him so much, you take him," said Fenris. "I want nothing to do with the worthless little poodle. Get him out of my sight before I kill him myself."

"Yes, father," said Warg who decided to take Skoll in as his responsibility.

- 7 -

Not long after that, the were-monster massacre caused by Lucifer's favorite happened.

Warg and Skoll had gone into business together. They were hosting a party to get the support of other non werewolf were-creatures. It was the first time in over 3,500 years all the were-creatures agreed to such a meeting. It was to get the various were-monster clans to work together. They were mostly leaderless and had no direction. But Warg and Skoll wanted to unite them.

And so they did.

They held a party and a feast in an abandoned warehouse.

Negotiations went perfectly. The food was delicious. And it looked like everything was going to happen. The two brothers won the respect of the other were-creature clans. They felt safe following the two brothers. That is, until the night was disrupted by Lucifer's favorite — Azrael. The boy Predator killed or maimed everyone there. He killed Warg right in front of Skoll's eyes.

"You killed my brother!" yelled Skoll at Azriel. "We will feast on your heart and your woman's heart and your children's hearts!" And then he ran out the door and home, begging his father to help him extract vengeance. But his father refused and begrudgingly let Skoll live in Fenris Tower again — being his only remaining son.

All the pieces were in place, decided Arba, as he manifested himself to Skoll.

Arba made his bargain.

He told Skoll he would help him kill Azrael and eat his woman's heart. He knew where both Azrael and his woman were. Skoll would then be able to show his father he wasn't the weak pathetic runt he thought. He could avenge his brother — the only being on the planet that had loved him. And with the full moon coming, Arba could draw upon and intensify Skoll's Lunatik urges to help bring out the immense power and strength in him.

But Arba needed permission.

If Skoll invited him to become one with Arba — body, soul, and spirit — Arba would give Skoll his vengeance and his father's love.

Skoll smiled:

"Yes," he said. "How does this work?"

"Leave that to me, junior."

Minutes later Fenris was alerted that his son had left the tower.

Skoll slew 13 armed werewolf guards — Fenris's most skilled and deadly assassins. The words "Fenris, your boy belongs to Arba and you are next!" were written in the guards' orange blood all over the walls and floors in the Fenris tower lobby.

Arba/Skoll howled then made their way to Belasco for the final showdown with Lucifer's favorite.

13
DEMON CROSSFIRE

"Jesus asked him, saying, 'What is your name?' And he said, 'Legion,' because many demons had entered him. And they begged Him that He would not command them to go out into the abyss."

- Luke, Divinely Inspired
Luke 8:30-31

- 1 -

Azriel, Dotty, and Roper explored Belasco for three days.

They looked for signs of what had happened, clues of where Finius went, and for information on how to send demons back to the abyss — if that was even possible.

All the monsters in town were dead either in the make-shift lab that used to be Pastor Shane's panic room under the church, or in the jail cells. The perverted troll and giant monster dog died shortly after Roper arrived. Most of the dead monster carcasses were dissected, mutilated, and amputated. Whoever had captured them was methodical and gruesome. Azriel and Roper had no reason to think it wasn't Finius's work. The slippery man had admitted to Azriel he altered his own body with zombie DNA and attributes. Was he doing the same with these other monsters? Kind of like a souped-up Frankenstein's monster?

The three searched every house, every building, and every square inch of town. They also searched the pit on the edge of town that used to be full of quicksand. The big triangular door to the abyss was not covered as Finius and Azriel agreed should be done. As they looked down in the pit, Roper and Azriel finally decided there was only one more place to check for Finius or other monsters:

The Belasco Woods.

But, they would wait until the morning.

"Finius is an idiot," said Azriel. "What was he thinking leaving the doorway to the abyss out in the open like that? And the safes with the zombie body parts are gone. He knows better than to awaken that crap again. This makes no sense."

"The missing zombies are bad business, no doubt" said Roper. "I can only hope they're somewhere hidden, buried so deep you'd have to dig for China to find 'em. But as for the door, that doesn't sound like any monster would have the power to open it without drinking your blood anyway."

"What do you know of the abyss," asked Azriel.

"Most people think it's the lake of fire in the Bible. Hell. But it's really just a holding place where the first eruption of fallen angels who came down and spawned all these monsters are now being held in *gloomy* darkness. Jesus sent demons there. There is a story in the book of Luke about how Jesus saw a man possessed by hundreds of demons. They begged Jesus not to command them to go out to the *abyss* — the same place those fallen angels are being held. They were terrified of the abyss and of Jesus sending 'em there."

"Do you think those demons escaped your house?"

"I reckon someone would have to invite them outside to leave. I didn't even know if it would work trapping them inside The Bunker. Pleading the *blood* of Jesus keeps demons away. But I didn't know the anointing worked both ways — on both sides of a door. On the other hand, they may not have been trapped in there at all, and just let me think they were."

"What do you mean?"

"It's how the enemy works. They like to lull you into a false sense of pride and confidence. Then, when the time amuses them… *GOTCHA!*" Roper slapped his hands together when he yelled "gotcha." "They could be here already, watching us, waiting."

"No," said Azriel tossing a rock at the abyss door. "I would sense them. I think we all would."

"Maybe," said Roper. "Never assume Azriel. Assuming makes an ass out of you, not me."

"Cute. What's next?"

"I don't know yet. But we should be patient. Even if Dotty and I can cast them out again, it won't be permanent. It simply weakens them for a while. They wander the earth. Then, they go back to the same host they were cast out of, while bringing seven more demons even worse with. People can be haunted by demons for decades — entire *lifetimes* like that."

"Show me how to cast them out of other people."

"No."

"Why not? I believe in God."

Roper laughed.

"What's so funny."

"Believing in 'god' is about as useful as believing in 'the universe' when it comes to casting out demons. Even the demons believe in God. They'll laugh in your face. Just because you can temporarily cast them out of yourself with your Predator tricks doesn't mean you can cast them out of anyone else. It takes more than just believing God exists. You have to believe in Jesus, everything is done in His name, pleading His *blood*, with the Holy Spirit dwelling inside you. You can't just *say* it, it's not a magic spell.

This ain't Hogwarts. You can't punch and kick your way to salvation, either. This is power that comes from above."

"So what's your plan if they do come back."

"Only pleading His blood can stop them," said Roper to himself, ignoring Azriel's question, and lost in thought.

- 2 -

While Azriel and Roper talked, just a few miles away the Arba-possessed werewolf was slinking through the Belasco Woods. Arba took his time relishing the young werewolf's strong senses and pent-up violent anger.

How did this runt not do more damage?

How did he not kill more people?

It's like he was sitting on a powder keg of violent energy but didn't use it. He instead channeled all that destructive energy into drawing and art.

And it wasn't even violent art.

It was comic book art — *cartoons* about super heroes and villains.

And even then, the heroes won.

Gay, thought Arba.

At least now Arba was in complete control of the werewolf's body. His spirit was attached to Skoll's and they were one, with Arba at the wheel steering. He could not be cast out by man now. And with the werewolf's natural strength added to his demonic enhancements, he found himself strong enough to pull a large tree up from its roots.

The *raw* power he had!

It was intoxicating and like nothing he'd ever imagined before. Killing the Predator would be almost *too* easy now.

Arba smelled his prey as he got closer to Belasco.

All three of the people he wanted to kill were there — the Predator, whose stench was particularly fowl, and the old man Roper and his bitch daughter who injured him before. He hated all three. And after killing Azrael, he would make the old man and girl suffer before allowing them to die. He would peel their flesh off one *thin* strip at a time and feed his blood-thirsty host's body the scraps.

Even better:

There was a full moon.

The full moon's power helped Arba draw even more upon the terrible energies and hatred the boy werewolf harbored inside. Arba laughed into the night. It came out as a howl from his host's mouth with that unmistakable demonic echo. He then punched another large tree. It cracked at the base and toppled over.

With his body, Arba thought, he could not only kill Lucifer's favorite but Rapha too. And if that smug wraith gave him any more shit, he'd kill it as well.

As Arba drew closer to the town, just yards away from the edge of the woods, he could tell by his senses guiding him, The Predator felt his presence — both his demonic presence, and his host's werewolf presence.

Good.

No need for secrecy.

No need for stealth.

No need to be quiet.

Those were more Rapha's style. Arba's style was to attack head on.

"I'm coming *Azrael*!" Arba howled as he started running — over 100 miles per hour, nimbly dodging rocks, trees, and bushes — towards the town. "And I'm bringing a whole shit-load of pain and suffering *with* me!"

- 3 -

As Azriel, Roper, and Dotty strolled back to the church, Azriel felt that internal monster warning in his belly. Something was coming at them — and it was coming at them fast.

"They're here," he said, as he turned to stand his ground.

"Azriel, now's *not* the time to scrap with these things," said Roper. "We need to get back to the church. That church was built on holy ground. Those demons can't possibly get inside without being invited. We'll be safe inside there."

"It's not just a demon coming," said Azriel. "I don't think so, at least."

The feeling in his gut was the same feeling he got whenever a monster was nearby. But that feeling was attached to something else: a cold feeling of dread. As angry as Azriel felt, he was also starting to feel terror. It was the same terror he felt when the demons were inside Roper's house.

Roper saw the confusion in Azriel's eyes.

"Something's off kilter right now," said Roper. "Something I don't right get. We need to high tail it back to base, *pronto*."

"Love, come on!" said Dotty grabbing Azriel's hand. He didn't budge. His skinny arms were tight with tension as his body prepared to fight.

Azriel looked at Dotty.

She was so beautiful.

Her personality reminded him of his mother and of Kerry Ditzler, of everything that was right about the two women and none of their flaws. Azriel realized this was about more than just him this time. He had to protect Dotty the way he failed to protect Kerry and his mother.

Azriel nodded, picked Dotty up, and ran.

Roper lagged behind. His leg was still limping from the fight in his bunker with the demons.

Azriel turned.

"Go! Never mind me! Take her, be safe! *Giiiit!*" said Roper panting to keep up. His denim shirt and pants were damp with sweat.

Azriel didn't like the idea of leaving Roper behind. Roper was probably the only friend he'd ever had besides Marvin Worely and Pete Crowley and Kerry Ditzler — two of which ended up dead because of him.

He wouldn't let that happen to Roper.

He set Dotty down.

"Go, run towards the church, I'll catch up."

"Love!"

"Go! I need to get your father."

Dotty sprinted towards town and didn't look back. She was so in love with Azriel now she could hardly think of anything but his safety. And the fact he was going back to save her father, well, she couldn't help but think, even with Azriel's laundry list of flaws, does a more *perfect* man exist?

Azriel turned and sprinted — so fast he looked like a blur in the moonlight — towards Roper, and was upon him within seconds.

"C'mon, let's go," said Azriel putting Roper over his shoulder and running back towards town. The old man was unusually tough and skillful. The way he dislodged and dislocated Azriel's bones and laid him up was as astonishing as it was painful. But Azriel could sense the thing coming at them wouldn't even feel anything Roper did if they fought.

Within a few seconds, Azriel ran to Dotty, picked her up over his other shoulder, and sprinted for town, into the church, and down into Pastor Shane's panic room.

Azriel panted out of breath as he set the two down. He had never run so fast before. "What now?" he asked, hands on his knees getting his breath back.

As soon as the words left his lips they heard a crashing sound from above.

They heard stomping and pews being thrown around.

"I know you're here!" said the voice. It was half a voice and half a growl that echoed. "I can smell you, taste your fear... and I *like* it! It tastes gooooooood! The smell is making me huuuuuunnnn—GRAY!" Arba sniffed the air again and smiled. "Ah, yes, there you are. You, bitch girl, I am going to kill you especially slow. Roast you alive over a fire. You caused me a lot of pain when you cast me out of my last host!"

The three heard the stomping footsteps coming to the door that led down to the basement panic room. They also heard the demon-possessed werewolf's feet land on the cement floor right outside the panic room door, which they had just rebuilt a couple days earlier. A sulfur-like smell wafted inside.

"So much for the demons not being able to get in the church," said Azriel to Roper as he clenched his fists, ready to do battle.

- 4 -

Arba yanked the rebuilt panic room door right off its hinges and threw it to the corner. Azriel was waiting. He tackled the werewolf into the wall just outside the room, wailing on its face and body.

The werewolf looked familiar to Azriel.

Then he remembered:

It was the same short werewolf he let live in Chicago the night Granny took him to that warehouse. The werewolf ran out and threatened Azriel and his woman and his children. Azriel didn't have a woman at the time so didn't think much of it. In fact, he was going to go back to Chicago and finish the job, but lost interest when he made it to the Oregon coast and lived in sweet, blessed isolation and solitude.

But now?

With Dotty's life in danger?

Azriel went into rage mode. He ignored the terror and swung away wildly. His fists hit the werewolf over and over. Each strike was so loud and powerful it shook the basement ceiling. There was power in him he didn't even know he had. And when he finally finished pounding on the hairy fanged face he noticed it was mangled. Its eyes were closed. And blood — that orange blood were-creatures had — was everywhere. His fists were stained with it.

Azriel's body shook and his body pulsated.

His eyes glowed fiery red.

His breathing was deep, and sounded almost animalistic.

Roper and Dotty could see a light around him. It was red and glowing. Azriel looked at them as if to make sure they were safe.

"I think he's dead," Azriel panted, then looked back down at it.

The werewolf's eyes opened and a smile formed on its fanged face.

"You hit like a *bitch*!" it laughed with the demon echo.

At that moment Azriel realized one of the demons was definitely possessing the werewolf. He didn't know for sure before, but now it was obvious.

The runt werewolf body kicked Azriel off him, and sent him into the wall inside the panic room. It then pounced on Azriel, punching and clawing at him over and over in his face. Roper had his arm in front of Dotty in the room's corner.

Blood splattered everywhere and Azriel was so dazed he didn't even process it at first.

He went numb.

Even a predator-blood hopped up Fezziwig and Rood didn't hit *this* hard!

As the wolf prepared to deal the final blow, a couple of large, milky white, bare arms wrapped around his neck and yanked him off, throwing the runt wolf outside the panic room against the wall.

Azriel blinked the blood out of his eyes and saw *her* standing there:

The same Predator man-chick who tried to kill him in DaBeach — the one Roper called "Olga." Except, instead of wearing the obnoxious Green Bay Packers socks and Cubs hat, she was in a hospital gown.

"Not so fast, Arba," said the man-looking chick. She had that same man-like voice as before, but without the accent and with the demonic echo. "You do not get to annihilate him by yourself. We do it *together*!"

"I found him first, he's mine!" said the werewolf.

"And I just found you finding him, no need to get bogged down in *semantics*," said the man-chick Predator.

The wolf got up and stared at the female Predator body. She was nearly twice his height.

"Scram, Rapha," growled the werewolf.

"We do this together, like the wraith said," replied the possessed Predator.

Roper heard the exchange of words from inside the panic room and perked up. "Wraith? One of them is involved in this… dang nab it, this pickle just got more sour…"

The wolf pushed the man-chick Predator, and the man-chick Predator pushed back. Azriel felt his mind clearing. He jumped to his feet, ran past them, and jumped up into the church, hoping, and now *praying*, they would follow him.

He was their real target, after all.

He figured he was now caught in this demonic *crossfire* and would give them both a target.

- 5 -

Azriel breathed a sigh of relief when the two demons followed him up into the church instead of attacking Dotty and Roper.

Their desire to kill him must be especially strong to do that. They could easily have taken the other two hostages. But had Azriel known more about demons he would have realized they don't think that way. They can't appreciate how someone could care about another person. And that sociopathic attribute had, for the moment at least, saved Dotty's and Roper's lives.

Azriel waited until they jumped up into the church and saw him. He bolted for the door, but the werewolf, even faster, beat him to the punch, putting Azriel between the demons.

"Prepare to be deceased," said Rapha as he approached Azriel from the stairway door.

"Abaddon has a real hate on for you," said Arba walking towards Azriel from the front church doorway.

Azriel's eyes burned that red glow.

He knew he couldn't win this fight with brute strength. No way could he out-muscle these two. But, he wondered if he could outsmart them.

"Wait!" Azriel said.

The two demons stopped.

Obedient turds, aren't they, thought Azriel.

"Abaddon… you mean the angel in the pit?"

"Is there any other," said the werewolf.

"Are *you* two retarded."

"What do you imply," said the possessed Olga.

"You two alone are stronger than Fezziwig was when he was hopped up on my blood," said Azriel as loud as he could. He was yelling, hoping Roper heard him. With any luck, he could get the demons to open the door and then push them into the abyss like he did Fezziwig when they were distracted.

It was a long shot.

But what other option did he have?

Worst case, he could tackle them into the abyss, and go in with them. It wasn't in his nature to self-sacrifice. But all he could think of was keeping Dotty safe.

Azriel continued, "Why don't you just open the door and let him out?"

The possessed werewolf and possessed Predator looked at each other and laughed.

"That was the idea all along, sucker" said Arba. "Right after killing you. Abaddon wants you dead first. Priority number one. But thank you for caring. That's *sweet.*"

Balls! Azriel thought as the werewolf and Predator ran towards him.

- 6 -

Azriel had taken many beatings in his life.

The high school bullies like Todd Rawger. Todd Rawger's zombie cop father Chief Rawger. The sailboat-obsessed vampire Rood and his concubine Mara. His own grandmother. Fezziwig — the first Nephilim. And, even Roper.

But this was, by far, the worst beating of all.

It was like when Rood and his concubine Mara and Granny beat him within an inch of his life… only ten times worse. And this time, there was no Fezziwig to show up to help. He could hear the wet sounds of them beating on his flesh, laughing that demon echo-like sound, his blood frozen from the fear even as his violent tendencies tried to fight back.

But it was no good.

He was getting beaten literally to death.

The only thing Azriel had going for him was the demons were operating on blind rage. There was no skill. No technique. Just wild punches and instinct. Not unlike the way he himself fought. This gave him a small opening as he was able to dodge and parry Arba's hit and kick him off while grabbing Rapha's wrist, twisting it around, and breaking it. The pain didn't phase the demon-possessed body. But it did slow it down a bit, as the hand dangled, giving Azriel a chance to kick her off him.

Azriel crawled on all fours to the stairway door.

He could hear the two demons laughing and mocking him.

"Yes, crawl!" one of them said. "Crawl and then beg!"

"Let's kill his woman right in front of him. The werewolf inside me SO wants that anyway," said Arba.

"My lovely host concurs," said Rapha.

The two demons watched Azriel crawl to the edge of the doorway, drop down to the basement on all fours, and then crawl towards the panic room. Azriel decided if he was going to die, he was going to die protecting Dotty. The thought of her screaming in horrible agony as these two ripped her to shreds slowly over the course of several days filled him with enough anger to ignore the pain. If it came down to it, he might even have to do the deed and kill Dotty quickly, to spare her days, even *weeks*, of torment.

"Roper, Dotty," he said.

Dotty ran to him crying. "Love! You're bleeding! You're hurt!"

The two demons hopped down into the basement and headed for the panic room. They laughed and giggled with excitement. Their mission was about to be complete. Abaddon would be pleased this time.

"Where's your dad?" asked Azriel looking around the room as Dotty stroked his bleeding forehead.

Roper was no longer in the room.

- 7 -

Dotty looked up, shaking in fear, as the two demons entered the panic room. The biting cold terror gripped her. She could barely move or even breathe. But as her dad always taught her, just because you're afraid doesn't mean you can't act.

She still hadn't eaten anything in almost two weeks. She had never stopped praying for protection and guidance, especially if the demons returned. Some demons could only be cast out by prayer and fasting and it worked before, why not again?

"By the authority and name of the LORD Jesus Christ I cast you out!" she screamed.

The two demons stopped advancing, dropped to the floor, and started writhing around. Arba grabbed at his face with his clawed hands. Rapha held his host's head as if experiencing a splitting headache.

Dotty said the words again and again.

And each time the two demon-possessed bodies convulsed and screamed more. They both curled into a fetal position and then went completely still. They looked dead.

Dotty breathed out a sigh of relief and smiled, "Azriel — LOVE! — I did it! I did it again!"

Then there was laughter.

The two demons stood up.

"Just humoring you," laughed Rapha's host. Arba joined in. "That was hilarious," he said.

"You stupid bitch," said Arba. "We are *bound* to our hosts body and spirit. We are one. We cannot be cast out. These are not *human* bodies."

"That's true," said an old man's voice from the doorway directly behind them. "But you can be *purged* out!" The demons turned towards Roper and felt burning, acidic liquid being tossed on them. The liquid was red, and thick. The old man was flicking it at them out of the end a dirty green rabbit's foot attached to a chain.

The two demons screamed in agony.

They felt like they were burning alive. Their screams had the same echo as their laughs, except pained and despaired.

They fell to the ground in the fetal position again. Roper stood next to them, flicking the red liquid on them. Wisps of smoke came off their bodies.

"Azriel, Dotty, scoot on out of here!" yelled Roper.

"What do you mean," said Azriel.

"Trust me!"

Dotty helped Azriel up and they made it to the doorway. Azriel limped past the agonized demons, spat on them, and kicked them both in the faces before he left the room. Roper followed them. When he got to the doorway, Roper smeared some of the red liquid — *a perfect shade of red, like that's what red* should *look like*, thought Azriel — on the doorway, then stepped on the other side and did the same.

Roper put as much of the red liquid as he could on the doorway until the rabbit's foot was empty of it.

The two demons crawled after them all the way to the doorway, still wailing in agonizing pain, stood up, and ran towards it only to be knocked back into the wall.

The two host bodies slumped to the ground, abandoned by the demonic entities — the man-chick Predator and runt werewolf looked dead from their wounds they had sustained fighting Azriel and each other.

The two demons were powerless now as they tried over and over to leave the room, but couldn't. That same force that prevented them from leaving the old man's house was keeping them trapped inside. Plus, it was causing them immense amounts of pain.

The two demons yelled and screamed, invisible to see, but were audibly heard. Windows and mirrors and glass all over Belasco shattered and broke at the piercing sound.

14
WAILING FROM THE CHURCH BASEMENT

"The nine most terrifying words in the English language are, I'm from the government and I'm here to help."

- Ronald Reagan

- 1 -

"What just happened," said Azriel shouting over the sounds of the two trapped demons wailing in agony. Hearing them trapped and screaming out in pain gave the three a feeling of impending doom throughout their bodies.

"Trapped like flies in a jar," said Roper. "Let's sca-daddle on out of here. These two give me the heeby-jeebies."

"I don't get it. They were able to walk right into the church. Even the anointing couldn't stop them," said Azriel.

"And with anointing *oil* that's true. They attached themselves to their hosts and were as one with them. They possessed non-humans — a monster and a Predator. It was actually quite clever of them. But there's one thing the demons can't stomach no matter what they are possessing. Something they hate and fear and despise more than anything — the blood of Jesus."

Roper held up the dirty green rabbit's foot on the chain around his neck and dangled it. "Thank the Almighty I don't need this stinky old thing anymore," he said tossing the rabbit's foot into the room with the demons. "Superstitious relics are more the *enemy's* toys, anyway I reckon."

"Was wondering about that," said Azriel.

"It confuses them demons every time. They see that foot and think I'm dabbling in things that will give them an opening. A *crack*. Something they can use against me. Sometimes the slower ones will even try to possess me when they see it but they can't. No room in here for anything but the Holy Ghost."

"So you anointed the door with the blood. Nice. How did you get your hands on 2000 year old blood."

"Let's just say it was a gift of love from a perfect stranger."

They listened to the wailing and threats and curses coming from the room. The voices sounded like crushed ice chips.

"Right now I reckon they're feeling a lot of pain and fear."

"Good. So now what?"

"Now what, what?"

"Someone let them out of your house which you anointed. Whoever that was will surely find them here and let them out and you're out of the Jesus juice. We have the door to the abyss uncovered and naked. We have monster carcasses all over town. And we never did find the safes I put the zombie heads in. Finius is gone to God-knows-where. This town is a sitting duck. What do we do?"

"Well, that there is a right handsome fine piece of a question, Azriel. I am not…"

Before Roper could continue they heard tires screeching and loud noises coming from outside. It sounded like dozens of vehicles driving into and around town.

The three then heard voices from outside the church.

Azriel hopped up out of the basement and into the church, and pulled Roper and Dotty up. Dotty looked at him with eyes he hadn't seen since the day Kerri Ditzler asked him to meet her in the woods. His face blushed. There was something unnatural and disturbing about how quickly he was falling for her and how she had already fallen in love with him without ever meeting him. It felt good. But it also felt like something wasn't right, either. There was a screaming pit in his stomach – his own "basement" – that was, in its own way, as disturbing as the screaming in the church basement, about Dotty. It was as if he knew he shouldn't pursue her. That he should get as far away from her as possible right now, cut off all ties. Maybe it was the demons howling below. Or, maybe it was something else, his own version of having visions. Whatever the case, he decided to ignore it for now and just be grateful they were all alive.

As they walked, Dotty grabbed Azriel's hand and smiled at him. The pit in his stomach vanished.

When they got to the door they saw the sun coming up. Over a dozen military Humvees were outside. Men in black suits and sunglasses were checking out buildings, guns in hand. Some of the guns were handguns. Others were bizarre looking rifles and hybrid bazooka-looking guns. The weapons looked like something out of a science fiction movie.

The man who looked to be in charge saw them and trotted over.

"Good! You're here, right where *he* said you'd be. We were hoping to find you alive. We're from the Federal government." The man flashed a badge. "I'm Special Agent Murdock. We're here to *help*."

- 2 -

"Thank God you're all alive," said Murdock. He beckoned to two agents nearby. "Put them in protective custody. Let's go, step into the vehicle, please."

Azriel didn't like the looks of them.

He didn't feel the monster-warning bells. But this Murdock guy and his agents in their slicked-up suits and sunglasses irked him. He looked over at Roper who nodded. The three filed into the back of the Humvee. The agents closed the door. Azriel tried to open it but it was locked.

"Prisoners," Azriel said. "They must be joking."

"I hate the government as much as anyone," said Roper. "But let's play nice until we see what's going on. The timing is very peculiar."

"If they do something to let the demons out we're fucked," said Azriel. Dotty shot him a disapproving look. "*Screwed*, I mean." She kept her disapproving gaze on him. "*In trouble*. What?" Dotty smiled and looked away. Azriel hated even swearing in front of Dotty and was starting to think she was stealing his balls as well as his heart.

The front door opened. Murdock sat down, turned, and faced them with a warm smile.

"What's going on here," said Azriel.

"We'll get to that. First I need you to answer a few questions for me. What's trapped inside the basement of this church?"

"You won't believe us, lad," said Roper.

"Try me."

"Okey-dokey doggy daddy, if you insist."

Roper told Murdock what was in the basement. He told the story of the demons, how he trapped them, and how it was important to not let them out under any circumstances or so much as touch the blood on the door trim. These were dark forces that can't be toyed with. Murdock wrote everything Roper said down.

When Roper finished Murdock simply said, "Understood. I'll be right back, stay here. We haven't secured the town yet. There are refreshments in the cooler in the back." He opened the door and left.

"I noticed you left out the part about me," said Azriel.

"Yeah, well, I am starting to *like* you. And my daughter here adores you. I don't want them to kill you."

- 3 -

"What do you mean kill me," said Azriel.

"The government has been recruiting Predators for decades. Every single Predator I know who's gone with the feds has gone dark. It's one of the reasons your kind is getting rarer, I reckon. Watch and see. The government finds you, offers you a lot of money and perks, you go, and are never heard from again. I hear tell the monsters are even more afraid of the government than they are of your kind or old duffer monster hunters like

Yours Truly."

Dotty grabbed Azriel's hand and gave it a nervous squeeze. He squeezed her hand back and smiled.

The front door opened and Agent Murdock came back.

"Your story checks out," he said. "One of my men literally just *shit* his pants in fear when he went into the basement. They have to wear earplugs. Whatever is down there in the church basement is constantly wailing and cursing and threatening. Don't worry about it. Nobody is getting near it to let whatever is in there out."

"Good, are we free to go now, lad?" asked Roper.

"You two are," said Murdock looking at Roper and Dotty. "But not Mr. Creed here."

"What do you mean?" asked Azriel. His temper was starting to flare. He hated being stuffed inside the vehicle and he just didn't like this Murdock idiot one bit.

"Don't worry, we just have a proposition for you. In private. You two may go. My people will drive you wherever you want."

"No, stay," said Azriel realizing his two companions were the only people on the entire planet he could trust.

"It's your call," said Murdock.

"I know," said Azriel, locking eyes with the agent. The agent looked away. Roper noticed there was obviously something about Azriel that intimidated Murdock and made him nervous.

Murdock put his sunglasses back on in the dimly-lit vehicle.

Douche, thought Azriel and Roper. Roper hated using the devil's profanity even in his head, but he couldn't help it. Who wears sunglasses in the dark?

"I'll come right out with it then. We'd like to offer you a job," said Murdock.

- 4 -

"No," said Azriel as soon as the words escaped Murdock's lips.

"You haven't even heard my offer," said Murdock.

"And I don't need to. Let's not fu — *mess* around," said Azriel, feeling Dotty's glance as soon as he began to say "fuck." He continued, "You know who and what I am. Even my last name. Just like you somehow knew to be here, in this town, at this exact time. Since you're the government, you're gonna lie. I get that. But I heard Predators who come work for you guys end up dead or missing or both. Why the actual hell would I want any part of that?"

"Fair enough," said Murdock. "Yes, we received an anonymous phone call about this town and what was going on here a few hours ago. We were told there were monsters everywhere. That three people who fit your description were in trouble. That there was something evil and deadly here and that we would want to know about it. The person also said who you were, what you were, and what you've done. You killed an entire town of people, Mr. Creed. You're the only person in Belasco who is unaccounted for and you fled, went into hiding. You're implicated in the murders of everyone who used to live in this town by arson — including three town police officers, the police chief's son, your own mother, and of Mina Harvey who was last seen with you almost 16 months ago in Chicago. We are duty-bound to arrest you. What if word got out that we let a mass murderer go? Or, you could resist arrest and be hunted by us. We both know that wouldn't go well with you or us. We are realists Mr. Creed. We know what happened. Everything. But even the best defense could never spin away all the deaths. The public would demand your head. What jury would believe monsters did it? But we don't want to arrest you or blackmail you. We want to *help* you. Help us help you help everyone."

"How?"

"We're on the verge of something big right now. We have a way to destroy every single monster on the planet without affecting even one human life and without anyone having to admit to the general population monsters exist. And we need your help."

"How is that?" asked Azriel. "Or, let me guess, that's classified."

"Actually yes."

"See, that there answer is why We The People have trust issues," said Roper.

Murdock breathed out a sigh and took off his sunglasses.

"Listen," he said, "What I'm about to say stays in this vehicle. It doesn't go anywhere else, understood? I could lose my job telling you what I have already. But I get it. I really do. Uncle Sam fucks Americans in the ass every day and then calls it *romance*. Learning to lie with a straight face is practically a requirement at the academy. So I get it. This is why I'm being *straight* with you Azriel. Our scientists are cooking up a virus. A virus that will kill every single monster, without harming any of the rest of us. We simply need more live specimens to study. That's what we want you for. We've been working on this for a long time and we're close."

\- 5 -

"Virus..." said Azriel. "How will that work, exactly."

"We're still figuring that out. It's in the very early stages. What I can tell you is, we need more live monster specimens. We need someone like you to hunt them down and bring them back to us alive. You'll be paid a lot for your help, of course. We don't expect you to work free. And from what I understand you *enjoy* your work."

"So," said Azriel.

"So you won't have to be on the run. We'll protect you from your past. We'll expunge your record of any crimes. You'll be getting paid to do what you love Azriel. You'll be getting paid to make a real difference. To help save the world."

"How much?" asked Dotty.

Azriel found it weird she would ask that instead of him.

"You help us for a few years and you'll pretty much be set for life. We'll give you combat training and weapons — anything you need to do the job." Murdock glanced over at Dotty as he continued speaking to Azriel, "Don't you want to settle down. Not have to be on the run watching your back all the time?"

Azriel remained silent. It did sound like a good deal. Maybe even too good. He liked what he was hearing, he just didn't necessarily trust it.

Azriel looked at Roper who was shaking his head.

"Mr. Murdock," said Roper, "Whatever happened to the other Predators. The ones I know who took your offer have never been heard from again."

"Other than the ones who died for their country, brave men and women, they are all happily working for us still. Azriel may even get to work with them later, after they're convinced he's not out to kill the world. But mostly they like to work alone. As Azriel's file says he does."

File? They have a file on me?

Azriel looked at Dotty.

"Okay Murdock," said Azriel. "I'll hear you out further. But I will only do this under one condition."

"Anything you want."

"These two get to come with me, get to see everything I see, get their questions answered as well. They're my advisors. If I get paid, they get paid. We're a *package* deal."

"Agreed," said Murdock and then left the car to give orders.

- 6 -

"Azriel, this is a dumb dumb dumb mistake. I want no part of this," said Roper.

"I do!" said Dotty.

"Dotty!"

"Daddy, I love him, I want to be with him. Wherever Love goes, I go."

"Azriel, this is a dangerous game you play involving my daughter."

"Roper I know," said Azriel. "I don't expect you to be a part of this. But I could sure use your help and guidance. You know things. Think about it.

We hear them out. If things go wrong, you tell me and we back out. But what harm can it be to hear them out and see what's going on? If they really have a virus that can wipe all the monsters out, then I want in."

"I don't trust them. Not one bit or a wit," said Roper. He looked at Dotty. "You sure this is what you want?"

"Yes, more than anything!"

"Okay then. I'll stick around… for a while, at least. But I don't like it Azriel. This whole thing doesn't sit well with me. No sir, it does not. I don't care what proof they show. You can never trust the government. Ever. They always lie or have some angle."

"I agree," said Azriel. "But I have to see this through. I've been alone and on the run for the last four years. I'm tired of it. Everything is hunting me down. This way I get to turn the tables. And get *paid* for it."

That screaming pit returned to Azriel's belly as they drove out of town with a cadre of government-issued Humvees.

He didn't trust this Murdock guy and he still had a troubled feeling about Dotty.

Was he putting her in danger?

Should he tell her to go back with Roper and go on his own?

And even though he didn't say it aloud — for fear of the vehicle being bugged — he didn't think the government was up to anything good. He also remembered there were a lot of dead kids at Roper's house the demons possessed. They would need that cleared up somehow. So he figured he could investigate the government's offer, see what's going on, and maybe, just maybe, do a little good for a change… while getting paid for it.

"So what happens to Belasco, then?" asked Azriel.

"We're going to keep men here at all times," said Murdock. "You can rest assured, it's well protected. Nothing will be *slipping* in under our watch."

- 7 -

Later that night none of the agents guarding Belasco saw or noticed the floating shadowy torso and arms slip past their perimeter.

The wraith had an urge to feast on one of the agents he saw. It was a fat man drinking a giant soda. He had lots of fatty flesh on his bones. Yum. But the wraith didn't have the time or permission. His master was calling him and that was the priority.

As the wraith floated down the streets, blending into the shadows, making his way to the former quicksand pit, he could hear Arba and Rapha wailing from the church basement. They were in everlasting agony and desperate to escape their prison. The blood of Jesus on the door kept them from leaving and seared them like a hot iron just being in its presence. There was no resting. It was constant, even worse than when Abaddon tormented them in the abyss. At least during those times they would have breaks between torments. But this was what mankind would call *inhumane.*

The wraith couldn't resist seeing for himself. He slipped past the guards around the church. He merged with the shadows downstairs and looked inside the room the demons were trapped in. They were wailing and weeping and screaming. The guards in the room had earplugs in so they couldn't hear but still looked terrified. The wraith noticed the two host bodies — the female Predator and the werewolf — were not in there.

That's odd, he thought. *I wonder where their host bodies went?*

The wraith left the church and floated down to the side of the pit. There were Federal agents all along the pit's rim. But nobody was stationed right next to the big triangle hatch in the pit's center.

They'd be shitting themselves if they knew how close to having their souls ripped to shreds they were.

The triangle hatch slightly glowed as the wraith approached and spoke to his master Abaddon through the door. It was like talking to someone through a keyhole. The wraith was told to let the two demons remain in torment for their failure. Abaddon would deal with them again when he was released. In the meantime, they had Lucifer's favorite right where Abaddon wanted him.

"Leave Lucifer's favorite alone," said Abaddon. "Let him do my work. I have something special planned for him I'll require your help with."

Abaddon told the wraith to let the humans foolishly think they were winning. Everything was going according to plan. Lucifer's favorite would soon know real suffering.

Go now, Abaddon told the wraith. *Go to help* my *favorite.*

As the wraith floated away, he heard one last command:

Oh, and take a light snack with you.

The wraith smiled as he floated up to the pit's rim behind the fat agent, put his clawed, jet-black hand around the fat man's mouth to stifle his scream, and dragged him into the woods.

To be continued…

ACKNOWLEDGMENTS

Of the three Enoch Wars books so far, this was the easiest to write and the hardest to edit. To produce it, I had to try to "think" like a demon which took me to some dark places, let me tell ya.

As usual, special thanks to my editor, publisher, and friend Greg Perry. If it weren't for him I never would have started writing these books at all. And, to be blunt, I write these books for him and me. If anyone else enjoys them great! If not, well, at least Greg and I enjoyed them…

My influences on this subject will be obvious to some.

Eagle-eyed readers will see nods to the movies The Exorcist and Paranormal Activity, and the TV show Supernatural. But the biggest influence was that dusty old Bible sitting on coffee tables and night stands around America. Everything you need to know about how demonic activity manifests itself and how to stop it is in that book. I suggest you read that for the hard facts and realities on this subject. I also drew inspiration from Dr. Michael Lake's book (about Nimrod) called "The Shinar Directive" and from some of the occult adventures (or, rather, mis-adventures) of Rev. William "Bill" Schnoebelen.

What else?

Special thanks goes to Jodi Ardito.

She's the best data-mapper I've ever met. She often has a movie plot figured out less than half way through. Thus, when I write these books I always ask, "will Jodi be able to figure out what happens?"

So far, she's been foiled each time.

Methinks she will be foiled with this book, too…

I also want to thank my dad Bill Settle and Stepmother Corrine Settle for being such enthusiastic supporters of these books. Every little bit of motivation helps! Same with the cover artist Kirk DouPonce. Usually he takes a few days to return my emails. But when I asked if he was up for designing the cover for this book he replied in three minutes and asked what was taking so long. Such was his desire to see what happened next to our reluctant hero Azriel.

Finally, props to my friend Guy Malone.

He ministers to people who think they've been abducted by aliens (www.AlienResistance.org) and I've learned a lot from him about how the UFO phenomenon relates to demonic activity.

Well, that's about it for now.

I think I already said more than I know.
Until next time…

Ben Settle
Bandon, Oregon

www.EnochWars.com

Made in the USA
Lexington, KY
01 March 2016